Duskin

BOOKS BY GRACE LIVINGSTON HILL IN THIS SERIES

The Man of the Desert
An Unwilling Guest
The Girl From Montana
A Daily Rate
The Story of a Whim
According to the Pattern
Aunt Crete's Emancipation
Exit Betty
Marcia Schuyler
The Witness
A Voice in the Wilderness
Duskin
Lo, Michael
The Sound of the Trumpet

Hill

GRACE LIVINGSTON HILL

Duskin

Fleming H. Revell Company
Old Tappan, New Jersey

Library of Congress Cataloging in Publication Data

Hill, Grace Livingston, 1865–1947
Duskin.

I. Title.
PS3515.I486D8 1984 813'.52 84-2021
ISBN 0-8007-1210-2

Published by Fleming H. Revell Company

Printed in the United States of America

Introduction

The cautious introduction of principles of sound guidance through Bible proverbs in this book seems to give promise of the strong emphasis on Bible truth that is found in all of my mother's later books. She herself would always have preferred to emphasize Bible truth, but it was not until book publishers began to realize that it was acceptable by a large public that she was free to include it.

The plot in *Duskin* is perhaps more slender than in most of her books, but it certainly is not the less gripping in interest because of that!

My mother was often accused of a belief in "love at first sight," and it may be not without reason. For even in this story in which the hero and heroine are practically at swords' points, there is a hint of first-sight attraction.

Villains are always exceedingly active in her novels, and they do not fail here to cook up nefarious schemes. As we look about today and gasp at the crime everywhere, we have the feeling sometimes that she had a "scoop" on the daily newspapers of this generation. The difference is that she had the answers that godless psychiatrists often miss.

RUTH LIVINGSTON HILL

Duskin

Chapter 1

Carol Berkley was still at work in the inner office when the men arrived.

Her fingers flew along the keys of her machine with the maximum of speed. She did not even hesitate nor glance at her watch as she heard the office boy seating the two visitors in the outer office and telling them that Mr. Fawcett was expected any minute now, that he never stayed out later than half past two for lunch.

She had been working at top speed since nine o'clock that morning. Her head swam and little black dots danced before her eyes. For Carol had been up late the night before finishing a dress to take away with her on her vacation, and she had arisen at five o'clock that morning to put the last things in her trunk and lock it before she went to the office. She was planning to leave on the Bar Harbor Express that night.

It was to be the first real vacation she had had in five years, the dream of her life coming true. Two whole weeks to lie in the sand and watch the rocks and the sea, a fine hotel in which to stay, and two girl friends to go with her. She was keyed up to the point of intensity with the thought of it all.

But these letters must be finished before she left, vacation or no vacation. And there were so many of them! It was like Mr. Fawcett to give her a lot of extra work on her last afternoon, as if he would force a whole two weeks' work into a single morning's dictation.

Mr. Fawcett, too, was going away, and was of course anxious to get these most important letters off before he left.

He was a hard master. Carol felt almost a tangible dislike for him as she drove her weary fingers on. He had been unbearable for the last three weeks. The old grouch! Of course he was worried about his business, for things were in a critical condition, but he didn't have to be such a bear. It wasn't her fault that he had got himself tied up in a contract that he wasn't going to be able to put over.

These thoughts hung around her like an atmosphere, depressing her.

There were still several pages of notes to be transcribed into the neat accurate letters for which she had earned a reputation. Her fingers ached and her head whirled, but she made no mistakes as page after page was reeled off and laid in its immaculate mahogany box ready for Mr. Fawcett's signature. She was giving her entire attention to her work, for she was deeply conscientious and she realized that these letters contained the crux of all the financial difficulties that the Fawcett Construction Company was now facing. Within a few weeks the issue, which was being discussed in some of these letters, would have to be fought out to a finish, and it would mean a finish to the Fawcett Construction Company if things did not turn their way.

Not that she would care personally.

It would mean that she would lose her job of course, and her unusually good salary, but there were others as good. It might be a wise thing to go to a new place. She was dreadfully tired of the little inner office and Caleb Fawcett's daily grouches. She longed inexpressibly for cheerful surroundings.

She was just beginning a letter to Philip Duskin, the young construction engineer of a large office building they were putting up in a western state.

The building was contracted for a certain date, and there would be a tremendous money forfeit if it was not done on time. Carol knew that this money forfeit would make all the difference between a pleasant margin and absolute insolvency for the Fawcett Construction Company, and she felt that the vitriolic sentences that Caleb Fawcett had framed that morning out of the bitterness of his anxiety were none too keen for the young man who seemed, as far as she could judge by the correspondence, to be allowing himself in the most inane and idiotic ways to be held up at every turn. And by such trifles! Rivets and paint and the like! Why hadn't he ordered his rivets in time? Why had he put the paint where it could be stolen? Stolen! The idea of a lot of cans of paint being stolen when they had been carefully locked into a room the night before! And even if they were, why didn't he get more paint, when so much was at stake, instead of writing a whining letter two weeks after it happened, complaining of his bad luck? And still persisting in that futile reiteration that in spite of it all they would have the building done in time.

And then that notion that he kept insinuating, that there must be an enemy somewhere working against them! Stuff and nonsense! He must be a reader of dime novels or an habitué of the movies! Things like that didn't happen in these sane modern times. Why would the Fawcett Construction Company have an enemy? They were an old respectable firm. The man must be a fool to try to put over such a silly idea on his employer. She had no patience with him anyway. As if a full-grown man couldn't look after a little paint, and get rivets elsewhere even if the first lot ordered had gone astray in delivery.

There was another thing too, why did his men continually leave him? That surely showed he was not a good boss. There must be something radically wrong about him. If Mr. Fawcett would ask her she would suggest that they fire him and get a new construction engineer, one they could trust. No wonder Fawcett looked so worried. It was plain to be seen that this Duskin was utterly inadequate. Surely there must be other men whom they had tried out who could take his place at an hour's notice, and save the day even late as it was.

But perhaps that was what Fawcett was going to do when he got out there. He was not a man who talked much, behind those shaggy eyebrows and those close-compressed, hard lips. Perhaps he had reason to think that this Duskin himself was the enemy he talked about. Perhaps it was Duskin who had stolen the paint and lost the rivets on purpose. Or very likely he had loafed on the job and knew it wasn't going to get done on time, and so was preparing excuses for himself beforehand.

She bit the words out on the typewriter with sharp clicks of her fingers, as if by punching the letter keys harder she could give more force to the unpleasant sentences of which she felt no doubt the young man was fully deserving. Why, here he was not only holding up the building for the people who were in a hurry for it, and engendering disaster for the Fawcett Construction Company, as well as hurting his own future career by his careless and criminal inefficiency, but he was causing numberless other smaller troubles. Here was even herself being held up from her long anticipated holiday to write this letter.

Then suddenly, she was startled by hearing the name she had just written at the head of her letter, pronounced in furtive syllables in the next room!

"Philip Duskin—"

Her fingers paused for an instant and she looked up, her attention drawn to the blurred shadow of the two men in the outer office thrown across the ground glass partition. One was tall and thin with a hawk nose and very little chin, giving his profile at certain angles, as he turned his head to talk with his companion, something of the outline of a fox's face. The other was short and fat, with full lips and baggy eyes and a shadow that sneered as he talked.

"That Phil Duskin has *got his price,* you know! I've pretty neatly proved that!" insinuated the voice of the short fat man.

The machine she was using was one of the so-called noiseless type, and the partition of the inner office was only head high, a mahogany and ground glass affair, which did little else but screen off one corner of the room. It was quite possible to hear everything that went on in the outer office, even when the keys of her typewriter were clicking at full speed.

For an instant, however, her hands paused, poised above the keyboard, a look of startled question on her face, and then as the import of the words, and the furtiveness of the tone impressed her as something that needed investigation, she suddenly slid back into rhythm and began to write again, easily keeping up with the somewhat detached conversation on the other side of the partition.

As the minutes went by, and the clock on the outer desk showed half past two, and then quarter to three, and still the president of the Fawcett Construction Company had not arrived, the visitors hitched their chairs closer together, and, it happened, a few inches nearer to the partition, and became more confidential.

Carol Berkley forgot that there were still letters to be finished before her employer returned, forgot that her trunk was locked and waiting, and that she yet had a few purchases to make at the stores, forgot that the rocks and the sand and the excellent hotel awaited her, forgot everything except that she must take down every word that these two men on the other side of the partition were saying. It might and it might not have any bearing on the case of Philip Duskin, but her conscience would not let her leave the words unwitnessed. When Mr. Fawcett came in she would show them to him, and then he could rave at her if he liked for not having completed the most important letter of all. At least raving was the most he could do and a few minutes more would finish the notes. There were only two more brief letters besides this one and her day's work was done.

The men were mentioning other names now, and chuckling quietly over things that had happened. Carol Berkley wondered whether after all the Fawcett Construction Company *did* have an enemy, as the young construction engineer suggested? But what could possibly be their object? Duskin's name figured largely in their talk.

"We could afford to divvy up again," they murmured, and they mentioned sums in hundreds of thousands that filled the girl with awe. These must be crooks on a grand scale and Duskin in with them or else she had mightily misinterpreted what they were saying. Her fingers flew faster, and she was not missing anything they said. Under cover of the steady click of the silent little rhythm they grew bold and talked more freely.

"Well, it'll be all over but the shoutin' in another month or so," declared one of the men, shoving his chair back with a grinding noise. "Say, when is that bird comin'? You don't suppose he's holdin' us up on purpose, do you? I got a date to play pool with a friend at half past. Better step out and scout around. Mebbe the old bird is out there somewhere!"

Both chairs scraped on the floor now as if the two men had risen. Carol could dimly see the shadow of the two, a tall gaunt one with a hawk nose, and a short thick one, with a bald spot on his head. One lock stuck up grotesquely as he turned his profile toward the glass for an instant, and pouted out a baggy pair of lips above a baggy pair of chins.

Carol paused, quickly drew the sheet of paper from the machine, and dropped it into a drawer beside her. Suppose they should open her door to see if Mr. Fawcett was in there and see Philip Duskin's name at the top of her letter!

She slipped a new sheet of paper into the roller and adjusted it, trying to summon her senses to a keener alertness.

Quickly she turned to the next letter and began to write. But before she had finished the date she was startled by someone in the outer office calling her name excitedly:

"Miss Berkley, Miss Berkley, where are you? Come quick! There's been an accident. Mr. Fawcett's hurt. They're bringing him up here. They want you to phone for the doctor!"

She was on her feet in an instant but even as she opened the door her eye took in the two men, and identified them. The short stout one with the bagging eyes and lips had been the one who said that Philip Duskin had his price!

She sprang to Mr. Fawcett's telephone and called up a doctor, found out where he was at the hospital, capably called the hospital and arranged to have him come at once. Then she turned to the big leather divan and cleared it. Among other things was a traveling bag open, showing a bundle of papers and a checkbook on top. How careless Mr. Fawcett was sometimes! She snapped the bag shut and swept all the other things into a corner of the room. She plumped up the leather pillows, and then turned on the two visitors who were watching her with significant looks at one another, and an appearance of waiting to be in on whatever was about to happen.

"It would be better for you to go outside and wait in the other room," she said to them coldly. "The doctor will want quiet in here. I will let you know later if Mr. Fawcett will be able to see you."

She stepped to the door and swung it open.

They hesitated.

"We're here by appointment!" the tall man said with an ugly

look like the snarl of a dog that had been denied a bone that was almost at his teeth.

Carol, haughty in her consciousness of what she had just heard him say, pointed briefly:

"You can wait out there on that bench!"

Reluctantly the two obeyed her, but as the elevator clashed its door open and the men from the general office came slowly bringing their burden between them, she saw the two visitors approach the aisle down which the little procession must come, and stretch their necks to see. Carol felt like telephoning for the police and having them removed, only that there was no time now to bother with mere criminals. There was need for her instant ministrations.

The president of the Fawcett Construction Company had fainted with the pain of being carried into his office. His gray hair fell back from his furrowed forehead, and the sour lines of his lips sagged wearily. One big knuckled hand that had always been so vigorous in its impatient gestures, hung limply down at his side as they carried him.

Carol was efficiency itself. She sent the office boy flying down to the drug store for restoratives. She brought water from the ice cooler, and produced a clean, folded handkerchief to bathe his face and lips. She adjusted the pillows and started the electric fan.

The doctor came almost immediately, but the injured man's eyes had opened wonderingly, just before he came, looked about the office uncomprehendingly and then intelligently.

"I'm quite all right!" he snapped. "I've got to go in a few minutes. Have you got those letters done, Miss Berkley? If you'll bring them I can sign them while I lie here and rest a minute. It was that cursed car ran into us. I'll be all right in a minute."

His voice trailed off weakly and he almost faded out again, but the doctor knelt by his side and wafted something pungent before his face:

"You're all right, Mr. Fawcett," he said in his cool voice. "Steady, there, steady! I wouldn't sign any letters just now. Let them wait a bit till I see what you've done to yourself."

"But I've *got* to!" demanded Fawcett excitedly, trying to raise his head and failing miserably. "I'm going to leave on the six o'clock train, and those letters *must be signed!*"

"Steady, there, my dear fellow! There's plenty of time. And you're not going to leave on any train—not today. I'm sorry, but you've got a little vacation coming to you, friend, and I'm afraid you've got to take it in bed this time."

"But I can't, doctor, I tell you *I can't!* I'm in a position of trust, you know, this whole company depends on me, and it will mean heavy loss, *irretrievable loss,* if I don't go at once and straighten things out."

"I'm sorry, old fellow, but I'll have to tell you the truth. You've broken the fibula near your knee and you're very badly bruised, perhaps internally. It might mean the loss of your leg if you attempted to take a journey now, even if it were possible for you to get about on it."

"Then I can get a wooden leg!" snapped Fawcett impatiently. "Leg or no leg, I've *got* to go."

"It might even mean the loss of your life, Fawcett," said the doctor more gravely now.

"Then at least I'd die honorably. Let me up! There *are* no bones broken. *I know.* I stood up by myself for a whole minute after the car was righted. I couldn't have done that if my leg was broken. I'm going to get up right now. Please all of you get out of my office; I've got work to do! Miss Berkley, have you brought those letters?"

He attempted to sit up, and sank back suddenly with a moan. The doctor laid a firm hand on his patient:

"Now, see here, sir!" he said in a tone which people did not lightly disobey. "I'm in command here. You're my patient and I'm going to be obeyed. Miss Berkley, will you telephone Mrs. Fawcett? This man should be in the hospital right now. He'll be getting a temperature."

"No! *No! Don't* call my wife!" said Fawcett weakly. "I tell you I've *got to go!"* he wailed, turning his head restlessly from side to side. "The devil will be to pay—it is now—somebody's got to get out there and stop it. Nobody else understands it."

"That's all right!" soothed the doctor taking out a little vial and dropping some dark liquid into the glass of water that Carol brought. "I guess we'll find somebody else to send. You can give them careful directions. We'll see that everything is attended to all right, my dear fellow. There'll be somebody—"

"There's *nobody!"* thundered the injured man. "Nobody knows anything about it but myself. Miss Berkley, you tell him. Make him understand that it is *imperative* for me to go. Tell him nobody knows the situation."

"Oh, you can easily explain the situation," said the doctor lightly. "I'm sure I can find a dozen people willing to help you out just now, and when you get nicely settled in the hospital and feeling comfortable and have had a little nap and a little nourishment, you can have a brief talk and give all directions."

"But I don't *want* anybody to know. I couldn't possibly explain the situation—Oh—h—h!"

The helpless angry tears were beginning to course down the strong old bear's cheeks. He was actually looking at his pretty young secretary as if he were a troubled little boy, and Carol Berkley were his mother.

What was it in his look that suddenly made summer breezes and rocks and sand and excellent hotel recede entirely from the picture and gave Carol Berkley strength for a sudden resolve? Something in the pleading angry eyes of her impatient old tyrant had actually tugged at her heartstrings—or was it that she was possessed of knowledge that he did not have and which would have made him all the more troubled and anxious to go himself? She did not stop to consider. She stepped forward.

"Mr. Fawcett," she said in a cool little voice that surprised herself, for every nerve was throbbing with a particular jangle of its own, and her head felt light and whirly, "Mr. Fawcett—*I* know all about things! Couldn't I go out there and do what you want done? I think I understand everything."

He turned from his boyish tears and became a man again, a big old cross tyrant.

"*You!*" he said, contemptuously, "how could a *woman possibly* do what I have to do?"

Carol laughed.

"I'll go," she said, still calmly, "I think I know what's to be done. If I can't make that man hurry up and do his work in time I'll fire him and get another engineer."

He stared at her blankly, the actual practicality of her words bringing him to see that she was not altogether devoid of sense.

"But we have a contract with him—" he objected; his brow drawing again into its accustomed frown—

"I know," she said, "but if he hasn't kept his part of that—"

A twinge of pain brought a sudden ghastly whiteness.

"Now, look here," said the doctor fiercely, "this thing has to stop! Whether this young woman goes or whether she doesn't go doesn't matter to me. This man has got to get quiet or he'll have a temperature before I can do anything for him. Young woman, if there's anything you think ought to be done, *do it,* and say no more about it. Get ready to go, and when Mr. Fawcett feels better perhaps he can talk with you for five minutes—"

"Oh," broke in the impatient patient, "I've got to go myself!"

"Now, look here, Caleb," broke in a calm commanding voice, as Mrs. Fawcett suddenly loomed up beside the couch, a comfortably stout little woman with a face that had been pretty once and a mouth grown gentle by long practice of living with a pettish tyrant, "you know that's nonsense. You know you're not fit to go anywhere, and what's the use of pretending any longer that you are. You've got to the point at last where you have to lie still and *take* orders, and you might as well do it pleasantly. Doctor, what hospital is it you want him to go to?"

Like magic things fell into order. The quiet stout little woman with the placid mouth took command, and Caleb like a lamb protested no more.

When the doctor had completed his examination and given his verdict, Carol was called once more to the couch to confer with her boss. Before she came however she beckoned to the doctor and asked him a question privately.

"Doctor, something has come to my knowledge since Mr. Fawcett left the office this morning which quite materially changes some aspects of the business. Would it be all right to tell him this? Or mustn't he be disturbed?"

"Are they of a disturbing nature?"

"I'm afraid they are." Carol looked troubled.

"Is there anybody else in the firm in whom you could confide?"

"Only Mr. Edgar Fawcett, his brother, and he is in Europe this summer."

"Do you think you could cope with the situation yourself? Do you know all there is to know about it?"

"I think so," Carol hesitated. "I've written all the letters; still, there will be great loss to the business involved if—"

"The business be hanged! Excuse me, Miss Berkley, but my patient has had a great shock. I doubt if the fracture he has sustained is the worst of his troubles. If he has anything more to worry about than he has now I can't answer for his life. You'll have to do the best you can, and let it go at that. But mind you, you make him *think* everything's going fine!"

"But those letters—" Fawcett was protesting faintly as Carol came back to the outer office. "They've got to be signed!"

"That's all right," said Carol brightly, "I'll type them all with the company's signature and put your name under, as president. I'll fix that up. Nobody will notice it isn't as usual. I suppose though you'll have to give me power to act in your stead. I've written this. I think it's what you wrote for me once before when you were away in Maine."

She handed him a paper neatly typed which would answer as her credential, and put his fountain pen in his hand.

He seemed somehow to take heart at sight of the businesslike sentences. After all, he had trained her, and she was an unusually good secretary. But how would she do when she was on her own? He drew a long sigh that seemed to be rent from the depths of his soul. How could a mere slip of a woman take his place?

"The papers are there in the top of my bag." He motioned toward the corner where she had put his things. "You'll find my wallet in the safe with money and tickets. I have reservations for the six o'clock train. Can you make it?"

"Yes, of course," she said crisply, "my bag is all packed you know." She smiled, and he suddenly remembered, and his face went blank. Perhaps he was not such a heartless old bear after all.

"Your *vacation!*" he said. "You can't go! You mustn't go, of course! I had forgotten."

"Nonsense!" said Carol with a quick gulp of renunciation in her throat. "What's a mere vacation? One can have that anytime."

As if she hadn't been waiting for hers a whole lifetime! For the rocks and the sand, and the excellent hotel, and her pretty new clothes—faultless they were, for she had been working on them all winter—and the two girls—But what folly!

"You want me to go straight to the building itself and find out with my own eyes just how far things have progressed?" she said in a businesslike voice. "And this Mr. Duskin—why shouldn't I carry his letter to him instead and tell him you sent me? Of course I know you were intending to stop over in Chicago—and expected the letter to get there ahead of you, but that won't be necessary now, will it? I can wire the Chicago people to meet me at the station with the papers, and ask those questions you had me write out. That will save a whole day."

He looked at her wonderingly. She did know what she was doing even if she was only a woman, and a young pretty one at that.

After all he found he needed to give her very few directions. Armed with money, tickets, reservations, and the other necessary papers she stood aside as the orderlies from the ambulance came to take her employer downstairs, and her eyes filled with unaccountable tears.

"Good-bye!" said Fawcett, suddenly rousing and putting out his hand quite humanly, "I know it's a raw deal for you. It's pretty decent of you to offer to go, but I suppose really the game's up!" He dropped back with a strange hopeless expression as if the worst had come.

"Oh, no!" cried Carol brightly, suddenly anxious to lift that burden from his tired face. "The game's not up at all. I'm in it to win! You'll see me coming back with flying colors to help you get well!"

He cast a sudden unexpected smile up at her, strangely sweet on the harsh old face, that was gray with pain now, as if he had cast away all pretenses.

"Good-bye, little girl," he said gently. "Thank you!"

They carried him out on a stretcher to the elevator. The doctor lingered an instant:

"You're a good little sport!" he said. "Keep the wires hot with comforting messages home and we'll pull him through. Let me know if you have any difficulties, and if you need to ask him any questions wire them *to me,* not to him! I can keep my face shut as well as the next one, so you needn't be afraid."

They were off, and suddenly Carol felt very old, and sorry as if she were going to cry, and very much weighted down with care and responsibility. Here but an hour before she had been reviling Mr. Fawcett for being cross and bearish, and hard, though all the time she knew he was carrying an immense burden, and now here was she with the tables turned, her vacation gone, and in its place Mr. Fawcett's burden thrust without warning upon her young shoulders. And besides that burden, she carried new knowledge that she had overheard from the two men. Then suddenly she remembered them, and looked around for them, but the office boy said they were gone.

As Carol turned to go back to her inner office she heard the elevator stop on its way up, but she did not turn back to see who was getting off.

Later when she came out with a sheaf of papers for the treasurer she had a vague impression of two alien figures, one tall and one short, moving along in the far end of the big room, but when she passed her hand over her eyes wearily and looked again there was no one in the room but the regular men at their desks hard at work as usual.

If there were only someone to whom she might turn now for a strong word of guidance and encouragement before she went out alone on this strange wild errand! Or, perhaps if she knew God, the way her mother did, it might help. She felt strangely alone.

Chapter 2

Somehow all the things got done, and Carol found herself seated in the sleeper, with a whole three minutes to spare before the train left.

She was breathless and throbbing with excitement. She felt as if she had been running a race with time, and was wound up so tight that it hurt her heart to stop.

Her mother and her fourteen-year-old sister had come down to see her off, and they lingered, wistful and apprehensive, loath to have her go. There had been so little time to explain to them, and they were still indignant over the idea of her giving up her beautiful vacation for this wild business trip into an unknown West filled with no telling what awful possibilities.

"Is he paying you extra for this?" asked Betty sternly, fixing her sister with a pair of very young, very modern blue eyes. "Because if he isn't I shouldn't go a step, even now!"

"Betty, you don't understand," said Carol, "it wasn't a time for talking about pay. I tell you Mr. Fawcett was hurt. He was very ill! The doctor felt it might be quite serious. He will pay me of course."

"Well, I should *sue* him if he didn't," asserted Betty indignantly. "Your lovely vacation!"

"Oh, I may get a vacation later," said Carol carelessly. Although the thought of her postponed vacation still hurt terribly.

"Yes, a vacation after everybody has left, and you're the only pebble on the beach, the last rose of summer! I declare I think it's the limit!"

"Don't make it any harder than it is, Betts, dear!" pleaded Carol. "Come, chirk up. I may be home before long."

"Yes, Betty, don't waste time blaming Carol," said the mother. "We must go in a minute, and there are so many things I wanted to say. You will be careful, won't you? Going off into the wilds—"

"Oh, Mother! It can't be very wild where they are putting up an eleven-story building!"

"Well, I suppose that is so," said the troubled mother, "but you—a young woman *alone!* And you're so good-looking, Carol. Going among a lot of strange men!"

"They won't be any different from the men in our office, Mother. They're just men, you know. And I'll wear a veil if you like, or dye my cheeks with iodine, if you say so!" Carol tried to summon a mischievous grin, in spite of the sudden misgivings that had come to her as she entered the sleeper and realized that she was really going.

"Now, Carol, do be serious!" pleaded her mother. "This is a dreadful world—"

"Oh, no, Motherie! It's a pretty good world! Wait till I get back and tell you all the wonders of the wild and woolly west beginning with Chicago. Just think of it! I have to meet the Chicago representative and talk turkey to him! I telegraphed him in Mr. Fawcett's name, 'Accident prevents my coming. Meet my representative, C. W. Berkley, tomorrow on train Number Ten and give her all details of situation.' Why, Mother, I expect to be treated royally."

"Mercy!" said her mother apprehensively, "to think you're grown-up and have to do things like that! I don't know what your father would have said to me if he had known I would let you go off alone like this. You've always been guarded."

"Exactly, little Mother!" said Carol with a firm set of her lips,

"I have! But the time has come when I've got to take care of myself for a while. It does come, you know, no matter how long you try to hold it off. I'm not a baby, and you know you really don't believe that I can't take care of myself after all these years you've spent on bringing me up. Isn't it almost time I had a chance to try myself out? Come now, flip away those tears, little Mother, and forget it. I'm going to have the time of my life out there! It's going to be different from anything I ever did, and I'm going to make a story out of it to write to you. There may not be any sand, but I'll warrant there's a decent hotel, and very likely I'll meet up with plenty of rocks of one sort or another before I get done. It's really going to be terrific when I get going, so don't have any more worries about it."

She forced a smile and her mother brushed an anxious tear furtively from her cheek and tried to summon a gleam of a smile wherewith to answer her. But the young sister continued to look displeased.

"I don't see how you thought it was right to disappoint Jean and Edith," she put in. "Did you tell them? Weren't they terribly upset about it?"

"I just had time to call up Jean and tell her in one sentence before I left the office. Yes, Jean was rather put out. I'm afraid I didn't make her see how necessary it was that I should go. I wish you'd call her up, Betts, when you get home, and try to make her understand. Perhaps you'll call Edith too. I hated to go with only a word to them, but I didn't have another second to spare."

"Of course we will," said her mother lovingly. "Oh, Carol, I put your Bible in your bag. You'll promise to read a few verses every day, won't you dear?" The mother's pleading eyes were full of tears and of course Carol promised, though somewhat impatiently.

"All aboard," shouted the brakeman, and Mrs. Berkley caught

her daughter in one last quick embrace and then they were gone.

The train moved out from the station and Carol realized that she was actually on her way.

For a moment she had an impulse to jump up and run out to the platform and try to get off. How *could* she go off like this into unknown responsibilities, and leave behind all the pleasant vacation that had been planned so long?

Then, as the train moved more swiftly, she realized how childish she was, after all her brave words to her mother. She deliberately forced herself to go over everything to make sure she had not left anything undone. It was as if she must keep on with the breathless race she had been running for the last three hours, or she would lose herself entirely.

The parting with her family was naturally still uppermost in her mind. How disappointed they had been for her in the loss of her long-expected vacation. It was almost as if they had lost something themselves. But how foolish her mother had been about her going off alone! And then insisting on that silly promise to read her Bible every day! She would have to keep it, of course, because she had been brought up with a conscience, but how annoying it was going to be—always having to remember that! She would not have time to read the Bible! Why was Mother like that?

Suddenly she realized that she was weak with hunger and putting aside her annoyance she made her way to the diner.

Most of the tables in the diner were already filled, but Carol found a vacancy at the far end of the car beside a lady with two small children.

Dining cars were not a common experience to Carol Berkley, and she scanned the menu interestedly, trying to appear quite used to traveling. After she had given her order she sat watching the children. She tried to adjust herself to her new surroundings, and to enjoy the experience while it was hers, but in spite of herself she felt disinterested, disappointed, almost ready to cry at the thought of what she was missing. In a little while now Edith and Jean would be taking the train together, laughing and talking, perhaps having an indignation meeting together at her absence. To think what she was missing!

She went over item after item of office matters that she had attended to before she left, telephone calls that Mr. Fawcett had intended to make before he left for the West, telegrams he wanted sent, notes for the enlightenment of whoever should take her place while she was gone, addresses that would be needed, a line or two about the policy that was being pursued in certain operations the firm was at work upon, things that no one but herself and her employer were familiar with. Yes, she had attended to them all, and had given the papers into the hands of the next in authority to Mr. Fawcett. The letters she had finished and had mailed with her own hand as she took the elevator to leave. She need have no anxiety about responsibilities at home.

She sighed a quick little quivering breath of disappointment as she remembered the pretty things she had prepared through the whole winter, which had been meant to shine at the seashore, and which were being carried into exile with herself, and would, most of them, very likely not see the light of day, or evening either, until she reached home and hung them carefully in her closet for another winter. It would have been a great deal better if she could only have had time to repack, and take some of her sensible old business clothes along. They would have been what she really needed. But it couldn't be helped when she had to go in such a hurry. Probably she might have had the tickets exchanged for a later train if she had only thought of it, for of course there was no particular point in her being in Chicago on time for that meeting.

She turned her attention to the landscape which was just deepening into twilight. A long crimson splash of glory against the horizon reached up through ripples of gold where the clear delicate green and blue of the sky glimpsed between. It was a breathtaking sight to watch, as the colors flamed and pulsated into one another, flecked from gold to orchid, and darkened into deep purple like velvet with golden rents. She was almost sorry when her order came and she had to give her attention to eating. The next moment they swept into a village with streetlights flaring garishly along the way and blotting out the wonders of the sunset.

Reluctantly she left the cheerful neighborliness of the diner and made her way back to her place in the sleeper. It seemed lonely back in the green shrouded compartment where the porter had placed her when she entered the train.

Yet she realized that she must not think of that for there was still her campaign at the Chicago station to plan. She must have some preconsidered words ready for the Chicago manager, must drill her mind on certain points that needed to be brought out, and certain others that were better not mentioned. There would be time enough later to plan for meeting the Duskin person. She felt that he was going to be rather an easy proposition. She remembered that she had always been able to use a keen sarcasm on occasion, and armed with this and with the letter which had been couched by her employer in phrases dipped in vitriol, she felt that she would have little trouble in putting him in his place.

This Chicago man, however, was quite another proposition. She knew him to be a nephew of Mr. Fawcett, a man of wealth and culture, young and therefore domineering, feeling privileged to dictate even to his uncle on occasion. It was going to be quite a trying interview. She realized that she must act the part of one much older and wiser than she knew herself to be if she would carry out Mr. Fawcett's wishes, and accomplish her mission, which was, to pave the way for a further loan from several wealthy stockholders who lived in Chicago. It was going to be like stepping out upon thin ice, and she realized she must go with determination yet glide with gossamer tread. If she put it across it was going to be the greatest thing she had ever done, just from the standpoint of her own soul, if nothing else. As she reflected upon the matter she was filled with grave misgivings, and more and more she shrank from the ordeal before her.

She slid over by the window, putting her elbow on the sill and resting her head wearily on her hand, her eyes staring out into the hurrying darkness that was stabbed with occasional lights.

By and by a thread of a moon appeared over the dark rim of a mountain, and glimpsed down upon her with a startling seeming of personality, as if it were wondering what she was doing off here, hurrying west. With a tug of her heartstrings she thought of that same moon shining on far stretches of ocean, silvering great rocks and wide white sand. Ever since she had planned to go on that vacation she had thought of the moon as going too. And now here was the moon, looking down upon her! It gave her a less lonely feeling, as if the moon were taking a kindly interest no matter where she was. Going with her to cheer her even if she couldn't go to the shore.

But she must get down to work and think out a plan for her interview with that young Fawcett. The better she knew her part the sooner she could conclude it and hurry on to the other part of her journey.

So she got out pencil and notebook and began to jot down several points that Mr. Fawcett had emphasized in those few minutes of interview the doctor had allowed them.

She had worked away for fifteen minutes on this and had resorted once more to staring out into the darkness, when suddenly she heard a voice just behind her ear which startled her with an unpleasant memory:

"Well, I guess this is our stall, isn't it? Number ten, that's what the ticket says," the voice shouted above the monotonous babble of the train.

Two figures suddenly towered over her; one reached across her and thumped a big suitcase and a bag heavily under the seat beside her shiny hatbox and Mr. Fawcett's briefcase. Then they sat down together on the seat opposite, and eyed her with open satisfaction.

It was inevitable that she should look up and face them for an instant as she moved to make room for their feet. When she saw them thus at close range her soul was filled with dismay. They were the two men who had sat in the outer office early in the afternoon and carried on that terrible conversation, her notes of which were at that instant reposing in the briefcase.

The tall one was chewing a toothpick and studying her face with a cunning interest. The stout one was sitting opposite her, his fingers caressing fondly a couple of fat black cigars in his vest pocket. He seemed to be about to speak to her familiarly.

She shrank away from his stout knees in their checked trousers as if he had been a leopard, and quickly turned her gaze out of the window once more. Her heart was beating wildly, and dismay had seized her. Could it be possible that these two men had to share that compartment with her all the way to Chicago? Would she have to stand that? She hated, actually loathed those two men, with their iniquitous hearts and their dirty tongues and their intimate glances. She had enough evidence in that briefcase to put them both in jail. Could it be possible that they had recognized her as from the office, or were their glances merely curious and impudent?

Her mother's words at parting came suddenly to mind: "You are so good-looking, Carol—going among a lot of strange men!" She almost shuddered visibly. Why were mothers always so farseeing? Why did everything they prophesied always come true somehow? And these were men whom she had good cause to fear!

Well, she had boasted that she was able to take care of herself. She had said the time had come for her to be on her own, and she must prove the truth of her words. She must handle this situation directly. She must hold herself from looking shaken. She must not let her lips tremble as she felt they were doing this minute.

She pressed her fingers hard against them and stared up at the moon. She could feel the steady stares of the two men, and it seemed as if she were a little helpless bird with a cat below her bough trying to charm her into falling into its claws! Each instant her situation seemed more impossible, and the state of her weary nerves did not serve to help her think what to do.

When she tried to imagine rising and taking a steady course down the aisle and out the end of the car that led toward the day coaches there seemed to be no strength in her muscles. Then there was her baggage. She could not leave that behind and how could she ever get it from behind the big suitcase and bag? Her feet seemed like water. Her hands were cold and trembling. It was ridiculous, she told herself; she was tired and overwrought. But the next instant she shivered at the very rustle of her soft silk traveling frock.

And so she sat motionless, her slender figure shrinking into its corner, and her face turned out of the window, looking up at the kindly moon. If only the moon were a person, to whom she could call for help!

She began to see with sudden vision how much more there was to fear than just two unpleasant strangers thrust in her neighborhood for the night. How much, for instance, did they know about her and her errand? Could they possibly have recognized her? And just what relation did they bear anyway to the whole situation?

A moment more and she remembered that arriving elevator

and the two backs, a tall one and a short one, that she had seen at the far end of the big office room. Could it be possible they had hung around hoping to see Mr. Fawcett or someone who could represent him? Could it be possible they had overheard anything as she telephoned?

Stay! Had they perhaps been in that little back hallway behind her inner office when she had called Western Union and sent that telegram to young Fawcett in Chicago, not only giving him the number of the train she was to take, but the number of her car, and section!

Certain words and phrases which she had taken down as the two men talked in the outer office suddenly flashed across her memory filling her anew with terror.

The far door of the car opened and slammed shut again and Carol lifted her eyes eagerly. It was the pullman conductor, going swiftly, efficiently, from section to section, taking up the tickets and putting them in a long fat envelope he carried.

Instantly she was on her feet. She stepped over the lank crossed feet of the tall man who sat on the end of the seat and flew down the aisle.

If her mother could have seen the glow in her frightened face, and the sweetness of her troubled eyes as she stopped by that gruff conductor and addressed him bravely, she would have said again, "Carol, you are so beautiful—too beautiful to go among a lot of strange men!"

"Wouldn't it be possible for me to have a whole section?" she asked earnestly, a wistfulness in her eyes that was not easy to resist. She was utterly unaware how charming she was, and how sweet her frightened voice became as she made her plea.

But the conductor did not look up.

"Every section taken, lady. Not even an upper berth."

Carol's heart began to fail her. She dared not turn back to see if the two men were watching her, but she was sure they were the kind who would.

"Oh," she said weakly, her hand slipping up to her throat, as if something fluttered there, "isn't there—couldn't I—perhaps—change with someone, and go where there is a woman? I would be willing to take an upper berth."

The conductor whirled upon her and took her measure with his eye. Perhaps he had a daughter of his own. He gave a keen glance down the aisle at the tall man and the fat man leering after her, and looked at the girl again.

"Nothing left but the drawing room, lady," he said gruffly, doubtfully.

"Oh, can I have the drawing room?" she exclaimed eagerly.

"Costs a lot more," said the conductor regretfully giving her his respectful attention.

"Oh, that will be all right!" said Carol with a great sigh of relief. "How much is it? Can I go there now?"

With utter relief she paid the extra amount, and went in search of the porter to get her bag and briefcase, a new anxiety attacking her now. Perhaps those men were wanting to get hold of Mr. Fawcett's briefcase! Perhaps they had been watching her when she put those letters and papers from the safe into it before she left. She eyed them from the shelter of the drawing room doorway until the porter had reclaimed her baggage and started back to her. But she kept out of sight as she saw the two men turn their heads curiously and gaze after him. At least they should not have again the satisfaction of looking at her. She felt as if somehow their glances had been defiling, and she would like to wash them from her face.

The porter and conductor gone at last she turned with thanksgiving in her heart, and saw that her berth was already made up! How good that was. Now she might lock herself into this little retreat and lie down at last to rest after the terrible strain of the day! She slipped the bolt with satisfaction. How wonderful it was that she had secured this spot all to herself, away from those terrible men!

She crept into her berth at last and snapped out the light. As she pulled up the window shade she caught a full bright glimpse of the moon looking down at her from a clear sky above open fields that were powdered with soft silver mists. It was not a thread of a moon now; it seemed to have come nearer and grown wider. Its light had a clear twinkle in it, almost like a star, that same friendly look, as if it were smiling at her.

She dropped off to sleep almost instantly when her head touched the pillow. Sheer weariness overpowered her. But sometime in the night she awoke suddenly and stared about her in the darkness. She felt terribly alone. There were strange grinding noises underneath and around her, above the rumble of the train. The moon was gone away somewhere and darkness reigned outside in the hurrying blackness. Only a few far stars pricked the velvet of the night. She seemed to be plunged back into an abyss of fear. The vision of the two men haunted the little space beside her bed and filled her with horror. She dared not open her eyes again to dispel it, and when she dropped once more into a troubled sleep she dreamed that her two seat mates were standing over her and laughing in her face, and one, the tall lank one with the toothpick and the bulging eyes, stooped over her and took her by the throat. She could feel his bony fingers clutching her, and she found no voice to cry out.

Struggling, she came awake at last to find a pale dawn creeping in at the window and a new country whirling by. She lay and watched the day come up and wondered what it held for her of added fear and perplexity.

Chapter 3

At breakfast the two men came and sat down at a table opposite hers, and seemed to take delight in watching her.

Though she kept her glance well out of the window at the new country which, but for them, would have been interesting, she still felt their gaze. It seemed to her that they were trying to disconcert her, that they understood she did not like it and for that reason fiendishly continued to annoy her.

She finished her breakfast sooner than she would have chosen and slipped back to her own car, leaving the door of the drawing room open for the convenience of the conductor, but drawing the inner curtain to it, and keeping herself well out of sight on the seat that backed toward the rest of the car. It seemed bitter to her that even the pleasure she might have taken from this journey into a new part of the country had to be spoiled by her dread of these men.

She took out the memorandum she had made of their half whispered conversation the afternoon before and reread it, wondering if perhaps she had misconstrued some of their sentences for she had been tired then. But no, they seemed more incriminating than when she had first heard them, and she put them away and began to ponder just how she should use them.

It was a serious thing of course to make a charge against them, especially so grave a charge as the evidence she held made necessary. And she was a girl alone, with no one whom she dared trust to advise her. If Mr. Fawcett had only been well it would have been a simple enough matter to have handed him the sheets on which she had typed their conversation, and turn the whole thing over to him. But here she was in Mr. Fawcett's place, possessed of knowledge that no one else in the company knew, and sworn to act according to her best judgment in everything regarding the Fawcett Construction Company.

Should she have consulted someone in the office before she left? Her judgment told her no. She tried to think of one who could have been trusted with the information. Mr. Clough the bookkeeper would have been for having the men arrested without further ado, and perhaps that was what should have been done. If she only knew! And yet on the other hand, it might have been disastrous to precipitate matters if it should turn out that these men were in the confidence of the owner, for instance.

It seemed to her that really the first thing she ought to do was find out who the men were, where they lived, and what relation they sustained to the matter. And how was she to go about it? Perhaps she had better telegraph tonight to the office boy and get him to wire the names of the two men. Their cards would likely be at the desk by the elevator, or perhaps lying on Mr. Fawcett's desk. Harry was a smart boy. She would say: "Send all information possible about two men you brought to the office yesterday at two o'clock. Wire answer care Duskin." Then perhaps it would be there when she arrived. That would help greatly. Only where then would the two men be? Her birds might be already flown. Well, it was the best she could do. Perhaps she might get some clue in Chicago that would make things plainer, or she might even find it wise to ask the younger Fawcett's advice. One thing was certain, she did not intend to give those men any more opportunities of seeing her than was necessary. To this end she managed to watch their movements, from the shelter of her curtain, and when she saw them get up and go to the smoking room, their hands obviously searching for cigars in their upper pockets, she drew a long breath and relaxed her vigilance.

The men had to pass her door to go to the diner, and she kept a diligent watch on their movements when it came near mealtime, knew when they went to the diner and when they returned to their seats, and timed her own meals accordingly, so that she did not again come in direct contact with them. But she could not get them out of her mind. They were like carrion crows that continued to hang over her head.

The afternoon's monotony was broken by a telegram which the porter brought to her. As she took it she noticed with eyes that were business-wise, that the envelope had been torn open, and she gave the porter a questioning glance:

"It's been opened?"

"Yes, Miss," the porter apologized, "the gen'leman, he done make a mistake. He expected it were fer him. He send his regrets. Gen'leman back where you was last night, Miss. He see the number of the section on the emvelope an' take it the message was fer him."

Carol felt a sinister apprehension stealing over her. Those men again! They had managed to read her telegram!

She gave the porter a tip and got rid of him, but her heart felt uneasy as she opened the telegram and read:

C. W. Berkley,
Section 12, Car 2,
Train No. 10,
Chicago Limited.

Dinner tonight, 8:30 in Fawcett's honor. You must arrange to stay over and take his place. Speech expected. Great opportunity. Several important men to be present. Will board train half hour out of Chicago.

Signed, Frederick Fawcett.

Carol sat in a daze and stared at that telegram. Well, at least there was nothing there that would give any information to those two prying men! But what kind of a situation was she in now? She couldn't stay over and attend a dinner with a lot of men! Didn't they know she was a woman?

She examined the telegram, but found no Mr. or Miss on either message or envelope, just her initials. Hadn't she said Miss in her telegram?

Surely, they wouldn't expect a woman to speak, yet the telegram that she had sent from the office gave all reason to suppose that the coming representative was fully capable of taking Fawcett's place. What should she do? She grew hot and cold, and a constriction of fright came in her throat. Ah, now indeed she saw clearly that her mother had been right and this was no situation for Carol Berkley to be in!

Gradually, however, out of the daze and horror her thoughts began to clear as she read and reread that message. Certain catchwords stuck in her mind "His representative!" "Great opportunity!" and "Several important men present!" Ideas began to shape themselves in her thoughts. She began to wish she were a man, and could make a speech to those men whom her employer had so earnestly desired to influence in favor of the company. Loyalty to her cause which she had not known she possessed came to the front. Her business mind longed to be able to use this opportunity. Of course she couldn't. Of course she wouldn't! But she wished it were possible all the same. She began to set about planning a speech for Frederick Fawcett to make in her place. She would outline to him several of the things she had heard Mr. Fawcett discuss with his brother Edgar before the latter left for abroad.

She began jotting them down on a pad, and as she wrote other ideas came to her, and strangely, a funny story that had been told in connection with one of the items. Well, she couldn't put that down. She mustn't furnish wit as well as wisdom for this speech. If she knew Frederick Fawcett at all—though she had seen him but once briefly when he visited the office a year before—he was not the kind of man who would want a speech written for him, though of course he would not resent a few facts jotted down.

When he came on the train she would give them to him and say that she must go on her way that night. She would get right into the subject she had come to talk about and when she was through he ought to have plenty of material for a speech. He was a Fawcett and it was his dinner, let him attend to it. She was only here to furnish facts and straighten out tangles. Of course, when he saw that she was a girl he would not urge her. He would be glad to have her refuse. But it really was amusing that he had taken her for a man. How Betty would enjoy that! It would furnish good material for the letter she meant to write home tomorrow.

The items to be incorporated in Mr. Frederick Fawcett's speech were neatly tabulated and ready for him long before the landscape began to indicate that Chicago might be in the offing, and Carol had made herself as immaculate as it is possible to do on board a train, and was ready for her interview. An overwhelming sense of her responsibility began to come down upon her the last half hour of her wait, and she wished numberless times that she had never come, yet withal there was an eagerness to make good and represent Mr. Fawcett as well as possible.

The train paused for just an instant in a well populated town, and then hurried on again. Carol pressed her face against the windowpane and tried to see if anyone was getting on, but could not discover. She finally decided they had not reached the right station yet. She sat watching the little villages go by, and wishing the ordeal over, rehearsing carefully what she meant to say at first, and how she would make it very plain that there was no possibility whatever of her staying to that dinner. There was no need for her to be on the lookout for Fawcett, because she had rung for the porter and given him explicit orders to bring the gentleman to the drawing room at once when he should arrive. There was nothing left for her to do but try to quiet her excited heart, and steady herself for the interview.

It must have been five minutes later that glancing out the door of her drawing room she saw him coming down the aisle to her.

She knew him at once and remembered instantly how she had made fun of his affected walk, and the way he wore his hat, and carried it tenderly, as if it were human and a respected part of himself.

Frederick Fawcett was a man of the world. He was accustomed to veiling his thoughts. After the first brief flicker of astonishment he was courtesy itself.

For Carol had arisen at once and met him at the door, with the cool little air wherewith she was accustomed to settle visitors who were too insistent to see her employer when he was busy.

"Mr. Fawcett!" she began when he paused uncertainly before the door, "I am Miss Berkley."

She left him no opportunity to be perplexed, and he adjusted himself instantly and perfectly to the situation.

"Miss Berkley! I believe I met you before in my uncle's office, did I not? I wasn't quite sure of the name, but now that I see your face I recognize you. You were my uncle's confidential secretary?" he hazarded. "I am so glad it was you who came because you will fit in so perfectly with our plans."

Carol felt that somehow her cool businesslike manner was being ignored and she was being put on the plane of a social acquaintance. Just why did he do that? Had he some ax to grind, or was she growing suspicious?

"Shall we sit down while I explain the situation, and then we shall have the preliminaries out of the way by the time we reach the city, and you can have time to rest and dress for the evening."

Carol caught her breath, and had her lips ready to stop him but he gave her no opportunity. He motioned her to a seat and took the one opposite her. She had a fleeting vision as she turned away from the outer door of two heads at the far end of the car craned in her direction, and the curious expectant look on those two faces hovered over her and hindered her in saying the things she had planned to say. Had it been possible that Mr. Frederick Fawcett had been in conference with those two before he came to her? He came from that direction.

Oh, of course! He had naturally gone to that section first to inquire for her. How foolishly anxious she was growing, and almost childishly suspicious! Then she roused herself to protest.

"I'm sorry, Mr. Fawcett, but it will be quite impossible for me to remain tonight, and equally impossible for me to make a speech if I could remain. I am not a public speaker. Of course you did not expect the representative to be a woman or you would not have suggested it," she smiled pleasantly and turning to the briefcase which she had open on the seat ready for use she began to take out the papers she had prepared.

"I assure you, Miss Berkley, it is all the more interesting that you are a woman, and a young and attractive one as well. This is the age of women. I think my uncle did wisely in sending you in his place, and I believe we are going to have a great evening. As for the speech it is not necessary for you to say much. We can talk that over later. I will just tell you what I have planned."

"But really, Mr. Fawcett, it's impossible for me to stay," broke in Carol in a panic. "It's quite important that I get on my way tonight. I must see Mr. Duskin at the earliest possible moment. Mr. Fawcett impressed that upon me."

"Mr. Duskin has been in Chicago all day and will not return

before tomorrow sometime," said Fawcett smiling, "so you would not gain anything by going on tonight. In fact it is quite possible that you may be able to see him this evening—I'm not sure."

Carol's face darkened, but she closed her lips on the exclamation of disapproval that she had almost uttered. She must not let this man know how utterly she disapproved of the other one. If he realized how inadequate to the job Duskin was proving himself it might affect his attitude toward the whole thing. Nobody must know that that Duskin job was in jeopardy till she had pulled it out and set it on its feet.

"Really, Mr. Fawcett," she said firmly, bringing forward the excuse that is always a woman's final refuge, "it's quite impossible for me to appear anywhere at an evening function. I'm not dressed properly. I'm sorry to disappoint you, but I came straight from the office. I hadn't much time after the accident, you know, and every second had to be spent in getting ready to leave my work."

"Oh, why, really, Miss Berkley! You don't suppose we're going to let a little thing like an evening dress hinder us, do you? We can surely beg, borrow or steal something for the occasion."

He glanced at his watch.

"We shall get into the city before the stores are closed I think and anyhow, if we don't, I have a good friend at Marshall Fields. I'm sure he can slip us in and somehow serve us under the circumstances, even if we are a little late. I'll telephone him as soon as we get into the station, and we'll go right up there. The company will of course stand for anything you need to get, Miss Berkley. You don't realize what all this means. I'm sure if my uncle were here he would say that you really must stay and help us out. You see this has been planned for a long time, and some of the invited guests are men of great importance. We have had obstacles far greater than evening dresses to overcome before we gathered all our guests together. In fact just now I had the good luck to meet with Schlessinger and Blintz, the men we're building that Duskin job for, you know, and I certainly want you to use your personality on them. They're being a bit difficult the last few weeks, and if we don't get done right on time I'm afraid we're going to have to pay to the last pound of flesh."

Carol looked troubled. She was beginning to understand how hard all this was for young Fawcett without his uncle there to help, and she realized suddenly that she had come on to take his place. Could it be possible that this was her duty too? It seemed absurd.

"But really," she said, looking at him earnestly, "you know my being present wouldn't make the least difference. In fact, I should think it would detract from the dignity of the company to have it represented by a girl. Wouldn't it be much better for you to make what speech has to be made? I had thought you might like to have a few notes of what I feel sure your uncle intended to say. It might give you a little different angle on things."

"Now, look here, Miss Berkley," the young man was very much in earnest, "please don't let's waste any further time in discussing this matter. You simply *must* stay. You don't know what a fine introduction I have planned for you already. Confidential secretary to the president and all that, the only one who was thoroughly cognizant with his affairs and able to take his place, and so forth. It won't matter a picayune after that what you say. A funny story or two and a word of greeting from my uncle and you can sit down, but I really must have someone there to represent the president who was to have been the guest of the evening, or it will be Hamlet with Hamlet left out. And I'm perfectly serious about the dress business. It's a necessary expense and the company will be only too glad to stand for it, and you'll be one dress to the good when it's over. Now, please, may we get down to business?"

Carol had a fleeting memory of a rosy silk reposing in her trunk, of another little affair of delicate jade velvet light as a moth's wing, with just a sparkle of sequins like star dust here and there; of a filmy white garment garnished with a silver rose; or would the little black satin with the string of pearls be more dignified and appropriate to the occasion? And there they all were tucked away out of sight in the baggage car!

"I don't suppose it would be possible to get hold of my trunk in time?" she said suddenly as if she were thinking aloud.

"Where is your trunk?" he asked eagerly. "I didn't know you had brought it along."

"Yes," she said, "it was all packed to go on a vacation."

"I see. Nice of you to give it up. Well, let's see what we can do about that. I don't know whether this train carries a baggage car or not. It may be on the next section. Even so, we might get hold of it. Have you your check?"

He stepped out and held a brief conference with the porter and returned quickly.

"He says there is a baggage car. He's gone to find out if your trunk got on. If it did we may be in luck. And now, what were those points you were going to speak about tonight? Had we better talk them over? Just to see if we agree in our viewpoint?"

"But really—" began Carol again, feeling that she was committing herself to the evening in spite of her best resolves.

"No, please," said the young man earnestly. "This is something you can't help. It's a part of the job. You have to represent Uncle Caleb. Now what are those notes you have there?"

Five minutes later the porter came back smiling to say that the trunk was on board and he had arranged with the baggage man to recheck it to the hotel without delay. He handed the new check to Fawcett who pocketed it and went on with the discussion.

"A great deal depends on that Duskin job," he was saying. "If that should be delayed, it might make hash of our plans. You see it's near enough to Chicago for them to keep an eye on it when they run away on business trips. If it gets done—"

"It *will* be done *on time!*" said Carol with firm lips. "That's what I came down to put over!"

She said it so firmly that she really believed herself when she heard it, and something thrilled in her heart and brain. She would get it done, too. Yes, if she had to get right out and help work at it herself, order the men around or anything! She believed she could do it if worse came to worst. It *should* get done, if human will could force it!

Young Fawcett studied her keenly. Not for nothing had his uncle put him at the head of the Chicago branch.

"You're all right!" said the young man fervidly. "Now, if you'll just say tonight what you've been saying the last three minutes, that about doing things when they have to be done, and doing them right—reputation of the firm and all that sort of thing—why we'll go over in great shape! I'm not quite sure yet, but I *think*—I'm *almost* sure—we're going to have Havelock there. You know Havelock? He's one of the greatest promoters in this part of the country. He's going to build a model hospital, one of the largest in the world, up-to-date in every respect. It's going to be one of the show places of the country, and *we want that job!* It's up to you to make him think we're the great and only construction company on this little globe. See?"

"But really—" began Carol, bewildered by all that was expected of her, "I'm not—I can't—I didn't come out here to—"

"I know," laughed Fawcett with his easy air of sliding everything off lightly. "But you *must,* you *will*, you know. You're *here*, you know, and Uncle Caleb isn't, so that's that. Here's our station, shall we go? Let me carry the briefcase. Yes, porter, the bag. How much time do you want to rest and dress, Miss Berkley? Would you rather talk before or after? I can arrange my time to suit yours. But we must go over those papers of my uncle's or we might get all balled up tonight."

Carol found herself being whirled through the strange city streets in a daze. She seemed no longer to have the power to protest. Some force stronger than herself had taken possession of her now. She had agreed to be its servant, and this was the result. She was being made to attend a banquet—the dinner had grown to the proportions of a banquet now, and relentlessly she was being drawn on to attend it, and to make a speech before a lot of men! It choked her to think of it, and yet somehow she could do nothing about it. Her trunk, too, had joined the conspirators and was riding behind with an air of disloyalty that made her half afraid.

She looked in awe at the magnificent structure before which they presently stopped. The excellent hotel of the seashore resort receded into oblivion before the splendors of this stately portal. She stepped inside with Mr. Fawcett and suddenly felt very small and insignificant indeed. What would Mother and Betty say when they heard how she was housed in Chicago?

As she stood at the desk while her escort arranged about the room which he had had reserved earlier in the day she glimpsed a glorified elevator in luxurious upholstery and bronze, and watched two men, a long lank one, and a stout short fellow in a checked suit, step inside. They turned about and she saw their two faces, as the bronze door clanked its noisy lattice shut, and they were lifted out of her sight. Her heart seemed to go dead within her. Who *were* those two men?

Up in her room Carol opened her bag. There on the top was her Bible, and she remembered that the day was well on and she had not yet kept her promise to her mother. It might be after midnight when she got back from the banquet; better get this over with.

A card dropped out as she caught up the book. On it was written in her mother's careful script: "Thy Word is a lamp unto my feet and a light unto my path."

Poor Mother! She was always doing things like that hoping they would get across.

Impatiently she fluttered over the leaves of the Bible. Proverbs. That was a nice impersonal book; it would have short crisp verses and not take much time. Time was going fast and she must keep at least the letter of her promise. At random she opened at the third chapter and caught at a verse:

"Trust in the Lord with all thine heart: and lean not unto thine own understanding.

"In all thy ways acknowledge him and he shall direct thy paths."

How strange! It was almost as if the verses were written for her. She put the book sharply down on the dressing table and went about her dressing, yet all the time in her heart putting up some sort of a wild little longing that the promise might be made good in what she was about to do. Whether it was all prayer, or part superstition, or merely a reversion to a childish habit, she was not quite sure.

Chapter 4

Carol chose the jade velvet, partly because it was the first thing in sight when she opened her trunk and seemed to revive her drooping spirits with its delicate elusive coloring, and partly because it was the grandest thing she owned, the only dress in her wardrobe that had not been made at home. It was a little bargain that a friend who was a buyer in a large department store had picked up abroad, worn once, and then decided was unbecoming to her sallow complexion, and sold to Carol at a ridiculously low figure. Carol had never hoped to own a real imported dress till this dawned upon her excited vision. She knew in her heart when she bought it that she was scarcely justified in buying a dress like this for the few times it would be possible or appropriate in her busy life to wear it.

But now it flung its delicate beauty at her triumphant. Here at last its justification was an occasion fully equal to the gown, and of course it was what she would wear. For a few minutes she hugged the thought to her heart. The money had not been misspent after all, for she needed something like this to carry off her part in the evening. Utterly without experience either socially or commercially, she must have something to back her up. She had always scorned women who depended for their success upon clothes, but now clothes suddenly took on a more important part in the matters of life. For if she had no speech wherewith to charm the guests whom she was expected to entertain as part of her job, no brilliant sayings to make them forget her lack of business experience, at least she could give them this luscious color to look at while she said a few simple words.

While she excitedly hunted for silver slippers and stockings, she almost forgot the two men whose sudden advent in the hotel had so startled her before she came to her room. After all, they had journeyed to Chicago in the same train, what could be more natural than that they should happen on the same hotel? It was ridiculous to think they were shadowing her. They were becoming an obsession. They very likely had no idea who she was. They were just a pair of rude men, somehow mixed up in the affairs of the Fawcett Construction Company, as hired henchmen likely, from somebody who had a grudge against the Fawcetts. Anyhow, what was the use of letting them worry her tonight? She certainly was safe enough for the present and so was her business. Tomorrow would be time enough to consider this case, and perhaps tonight she might find someone in whom she would care to confide, someone of whom to ask advice. But no, it would be better to keep things to herself until she could get a message through to Mr. Fawcett himself. Perhaps in a few days he would be better, might even be well enough to talk on the phone, or better still to come on by the end of the next week and shoulder the whole responsibility.

With this comforting reflection she went about the business of dressing with something like actual pleasure. Of course she was tired, but the excitement of the evening had made her forget.

She turned on the water in her wonderful white bathroom and thought how she would describe it all to Mother and Betty, this more than excellent hotel in which she was to be housed for the night. A telephone by her luxurious bed, lights in every conceivable corner where one could possibly desire to see, a dream of a desk with an assortment of important looking stationery of various sizes and shapes! She certainly would write at least a note home that night before she slept no matter how sleepy she was when she returned to the hotel.

Refreshed by a luxurious bath, and arrayed at last in the lovely dress, she stood before the mirror and looked at herself critically. She was startled to see how little she resembled the quiet somberly dressed secretary from the inner office of the Fawcett Construction Company. In the first place there was a radiance about her face that she could not in the least understand, like a child off on a picnic. Was it possible that after all she was *enjoying* this impossible job which she had undertaken? She looked herself straight in the eye and resolved to have it out with herself when she was rested from this evening. She must understand her own soul and its motives or she surely would never be able to go on with things.

But aside from the radiance of her face she was thrilled to know that she looked a lady, every inch of her, from the tip of her silver slippers to the crown of the red-gold waves of her shining hair. The lines of her frock were simple and perfect, and the light powdering of glittering specks was just enough to relieve the plainness of the dress. She looked like some lovely evening moth about to fly in the moonlight. The little string of inexpensive but nicely cut crystal beads about her throat seemed to be a part of the costume, and the lights and shades on the velvet reminded of nothing else but the bloom on a butterfly's wing.

But Carol was not thinking of all this; she was examining herself critically from the standpoint of the world. Did she look as a representative of a great New York firm ought to look to undertake the business of the evening? In the words of her small brother at home did she look "as if she knew her onions"?

While she was still critically, uncertainly, pondering the question the telephone sounded and a voice from the desk made it known that Mr. Fawcett was awaiting her coming.

With a quick glance into the mirror and a catch of her breath at the thought that she was about to go out on the most critical undertaking she had ever yet attempted, she threw her white evening cloak about her shoulders and gave another glance into the mirror with a tender thought for the mother and sister whose secret purchase the wrap had been. She knew the many trips to the stores they had taken in search of just the right thing, their glee over having found one with some lovely white fur on the collar. She had thought to wear it to the beach for the first time tonight, but here she was in a far off city, about to go to a banquet, and thanks to her mother and sister there was nothing wanting from the conventional costume that other people wore on such occasions. Feeling comfortable in this knowledge she snapped out the light, locked her door, and went down to meet Mr. Frederick Fawcett.

She would not have been human if she had not noticed his look of not only hearty approval, but genuine admiration when he caught sight of her. It gave her the confidence that she needed for what she had to do that evening, the part she had to play for the sake of her employer who lay ill and could not do it for himself.

That was what clothes ought to be, she reflected, a sort of armor for the fight of life. It was well if one could have good armor, and know that it fitted lightly and well and would not cause hindrance in the thick of the fight. She did not want to think how she was looking when it came to making her speech.

Coming down in the elevator had brought to mind the two men, but she did not see them in the brightly lighted lobby anywhere. She gave a hasty glance about the lofty apartment, marble-arched and palm-shadowed. It was a lovely place with nothing in sight to annoy or make afraid. Out the arched doorway there were two men in evening dress getting into a taxi, and one was tall and one was short, but the two she dreaded would never wear tuxedos and high hats! They were surely not of that class!

Frederick Fawcett had brought his own car, and Carol was whirled away to another great hotel, also palm-shadowed, marble-arched, and pillared in great vistas of beauty. Another elevator carried them up to a high floor, and landed them in the apartments prepared for the banquet. Carol's panic began as she went to the cloakroom alone, with a sudden rush of horror over what was to come next, a sudden startling possibility that she might be the only woman present among no knowing how many men!

Well, if that were the case she would try to act as if that were a perfectly ordinary situation, and keep her dignity and say as little as possible under the circumstances. She was a businesswoman on a mission, and that was all. She was not there socially. She would not forget that for an instant. Thus she armored her soul.

But Frederick Fawcett had not been born to the purple for nothing. In the brief interval between the time when he had left her, and the moment when he called for her he had somehow succeeded in procuring three other women guests for the evening, though none of them had expected until then to be present. One was an elderly cousin who was thrilled at the idea of getting in on a dinner with notables, one a young girl about Carol's age, and the third the wife of a staid and elderly bank president who was himself one of the original guests. Fawcett had begged the presence of the ladies as a special favor in view of the fact that the representative of the guest of honor had turned out to be a woman, and he did not wish her to be uncomfortable.

Carol drew a long breath when she emerged from the cloakroom and saw them, clad in hasty conventional black, but she looked doubtfully at her own soft brightness and wondered if it would be too conspicuous.

She did not know how lovely she looked as she stood poised at the entrance and glanced about her. More than one conversation hung in midair while all eyes were turned toward her, a distinguished and lovely guest indeed. Her mother, could she have seen her at that moment, would certainly have thought again: "Carol, you are too good-looking to be going off alone among a lot of men."

A young man, himself good to look upon, was standing not far from the doorway talking with a white-haired financier. At the general hush that followed Carol's arrival, he looked up and saw her—so exquisite, so natural, so characterful, and forgot what he had been saying. He had not known that the modern world still held a girl like that. For a moment he watched her, expecting her to dissolve into a hard modern siren under his glance; he was a bit of a cynic about girls. Carol's eyes were involuntarily drawn to meet his. Just for an instant her glance lingered, appraising him. He certainly had an interesting face. Then she saw him with his companion coming toward her and let her eyes go on around the room.

Up to this point she was keenly conscious of herself, of how she was carrying herself.

But suddenly she forgot herself, forgot the company of strangers, forgot that an extremely good-looking young man, in fact the most interesting looking man she ever remembered to have seen, was on his way across the room apparently in order to be introduced to her, forgot everything except that she was just Carol Berkley, the secretary of the Fawcett Construction Company masquerading as a representative of the company itself, and that there across the room from her stood those two awful men!

They were both in evening dress, but they had not changed their characters. The little beastly eyes of the short one glinted just as cunningly from his fat pink face, and his chins lay in just as uncomely ropes above a full-dress shirt as when he had worn his checked business suit, and the long fox nose and receding chin of the tall one looked even more foxlike over a white tie than over the gaudy red-striped one he had worn in the train. There was no mistaking them, but how did they get in here? And what should she do about it?

She looked wildly about for Mr. Fawcett but he was at the far end of the room saying something to the headwaiter about the arrangement of seats. Besides, it would not do to tell him now that these two men were crooks. She must find out who they were. She must be controlled, and do the wise thing. Here was the test of her fitness to perform her errand. These men must not guess anything from her attitude. They must not know that she recognized them.

It was as if the situation suddenly stalked up to her and challenged her there in the big archway of the banquet hall, before all those people, and told her to make good now, once for all or else own herself beaten and run from the place! She met the issue without wavering. She *made* her eyes pass over those two grinning countenances, rest lightly here and there about the room, and come back to the group of people nearest her. She *made* herself smile, a frozen little waif of a smile perhaps—but still she was among strangers and they would not know the warm pleasant lighting of her natural smile. She *made* her heart stop its pounding and taking a deep breath smiled again more naturally this time. Was she going to be able to put it across? She wasn't sure yet. Her head was whirling and she scarcely distinguished between the mass of faces that bobbed and chattered before her. Yet only a heightened color and a certain brilliancy of her eyes gave outward sign of her perturbation.

The exceedingly good-looking young man arrived and was introduced by Mr. Fawcett who suddenly appeared at her side along with the distinguished financier. But she scarcely saw them. She acknowledged the introductions with a cool sweet aloofness, but she did not hear their names, and suddenly the two men whom she dreaded appeared in front of her and Frederick Fawcett said:

"Miss Berkley, let me introduce Mr. Schlessinger and Mr. Blintz. You will remember I told you we were to be favored."

Carol turned quickly to face the two men who had seemed to haunt her steps since she started!

Schlessinger and Blintz! Could it be that she had heard the names right! Could those two unspeakable hounds be the two men for whom that troublesome building was being put up? What did it all mean?

She had herself well in hand. She hoped she did not look startled. She acknowledged the introduction gravely, with a certain dignity that held in check by main force the air of familiarity with which they attempted to approach her.

"Yes, we've met before I think," said Blintz with a knowing grin, the same that he had given her in the sleeper section before she hastily changed her reservation.

He was all too evidently waiting for her to acknowledge the acquaintance. Carol felt a cold horror gripping at her throat. Her lips seemed frozen past all smiling. She lifted her eyebrows a trifle, questioningly. There was almost haughtiness in her tones:

"Really?" she said out of lips that seemed to have lost their facile curves. "Aren't you mistaken?"

The man stared at her.

"We were in the same section in the sleeper," reminded Blintz with something that might have been almost a snicker in his voice.

Still Carol managed to keep that calm questioning look, lifting her brows again gravely:

"I believe there was someone else in the section where I sat first," she said evenly. "I was quite occupied in getting settled in the drawing room. I had to leave so suddenly that I had no opportunity to find out where my reservations were beforehand."

"But we met you before that in Mr. Fawcett's private office," insisted Schlessinger coming to the front now, "just as they were bringing Fawcett in, you remember? We told you we had an appointment with him, you know."

"Really?" said Carol again sweetly but distantly. It seemed to be a good word wherewith to bridge the chasm. "There are so many people coming and going you know. It wasn't a time to remember faces just then. We were all quite excited."

"Yes, yes," grinned Blintz hastening on. "It was unfortunate of course. But what we want to know, young lady, is what's to be done *now?* What are you going to do with that building of ours? The young man at the head of that job is being held up at every turn. I'm afraid he isn't equal to the task. And it means a great deal to you as well as to us if the contract isn't done on time. Do you think you can handle it? What are you going to do with Duskin when you find you can't make him get done on time?"

"Fire him!" she said glibly, looking steadily in the eye of the man who had said that Duskin had his price. "Fire him and get someone who can't be—" she hesitated just a flicker of an instant then finished swiftly in one clear-cut word "*—bought!*"

She turned quickly away lest she strike the lying lips before her, and in turning met the keen grave eyes of the young man to whom she had just been introduced.

One look he gave her, searching—disapproving? What was it? There was no smile on his lips now, rather contempt. Had her words sounded flippant to his passing ear? She had a sense of wishing she might explain herself, turn back and say something that would justify the stand she had taken. But when she looked back he was gone, stalking to the far end of the room. She dared not look at Schlessinger and Blintz to get their reaction. She was depressed with the idea that she had somehow made a bad beginning. She had been too cocksure of herself. That little bit of open admiration at the first had turned her head perhaps. She had been too smart. She should have bided her time and not attempted to answer back. Perhaps they were keen enough to have been put on their guard by her words. Oh, she had failed utterly, and right at the start! And that young stranger had given her a look which rankled in her soul. She could not get rid of the discomfort it gave her. Depression sat upon her soul like a sudden mighty weight. It was just as she had thought it was going to be: she was not equal to the occasion. She ought to have refused to come. How she wished she might even now steal out the door and fly down the marble stairs that were visible through the arch, and disappear into the street!

It was a relief when she was seated to find that the young man who had suddenly become so distasteful was seated far down the table on the other side, and that Schlessinger and Blintz were almost opposite to him and therefore where they could not watch her nor she them. If it fell out that she was still unable to elude that speech, she would be much less distraught if she could keep them out of her sight.

As for the young man, she decided to put him out of her thoughts also. Who was he anyway but a stranger? What had he to do with the affair of the moment? He was doubtless some banker or other who did not matter much. If she could swing the rest of the company into line she might afford to forget him—one young man. She noticed with relief that the one other young woman was by his side and he would therefore be absorbed with her. Very likely he had only been invited for her sake. She was probably the daughter of some magnate or other connected with the business world who mattered much to the company. Perhaps the two were engaged.

Well, she would forget him, blot him out of the picture as it were, and then perhaps she could go on and finish her part.

Oh, how glad she would be when the evening was over and she was free at last, free to go back to that quiet hotel room and that beautiful white bed and get rested! How tired she was! She wondered if she would ever get rested! She resolved to sleep as late as she chose in the morning. Perhaps she would even wait until afternoon or the next morning to continue her journey, if she didn't feel rested tomorrow. There was no such great rush of course if the Duskin man was off the job. There really was no point in getting there until he arrived and she could get down to business—fire him if necessary. She naturally couldn't dismiss him from the service of the company while he was away.

Then someone on her left spoke to her and she was swept into the tide of talk.

They were a bright crowd of people, even the elderly cousin who had been requisitioned for the occasion. The conversation sparkled with wit and repartee. It was a new and stimulating experience to Carol who had hitherto sat quietly on the outside edge of business affairs and approached only to serve.

These were people of large affairs, used to managing great operations, conversant with the big things of the day, who spoke of millions as she would of dimes and quarters, who suggested building libraries or hospitals or art museums as if they were gods who could command and these would appear. They discussed Herculean undertakings as lightly as if they were trifles. She began to look upon them with awe. And *she* was expected to *speak* to these people. To represent great interests and intrigue their fancy! It was appalling. Like a death knell this thought rang an undertone as course succeeded delicious course, through fruit, soup, fish, game, salad and confections. She ate the delectable concoctions as if she were in a dream, occasionally wondering what Mother and Betty would say if they could look in upon her, if they could taste these wonders of the culinary art, and witness the lavish display of flowers and costly viands. And here were these people toying with each course as if they were but the regular everyday bread and butter of life, rather than a succession of delicacies.

Yet she could not thoroughly enjoy it all, for there far down the length of the table she now and then caught sight of a dark head bent deferentially to the pretty girl beside it, and she could not forget the look its owner had given her. And there on the other side of the table, out of sight if she sat back in her place, but never out of mind, were those two horrid men with whom she must deal somehow on the morrow. And there, also just ahead a few minutes perhaps, loomed a speech she must make, and make it well, as well, or better than Caleb Fawcett himself could have made it, and she hadn't an idea in her head! All the fine points that she had jotted down so carefully for Frederick Fawcett had deserted her. Only the funny story was left, and it had somehow lost its point. Why had she ever thought it was funny?

And then at last the moment for the speech took her unawares.

The ices had been served and geniality was like a sunny atmosphere. For the moment Carol had almost forgotten herself in listening to a story that her neighbor on the left was telling.

He was an elderly man of wide culture and had traveled a great deal. He had recently returned from a trip to South America and was relating some of his experiences.

Across the table there was another conversation in progress which interested her immensely, and of which she caught an occasional sentence. The people were talking about Pennell's pictures and how he had been the first to find art in common labor and construction. Carol was interested in that because she had recently taken a trip to Washington, and spent several hours going through an exhibit of Pennell's pictures in the Library of Congress. She had thrilled to the beauty of the intricate network of steel girders towering up into heaven against the smoky background of the city. The artist had caught the lines of grandeur and beauty in even common things and made them live on paper. This seemed to her a great mission in life. Yet the elderly cousin who had traveled much and visited the world's great picture galleries was decrying the modern idea of commercializing, as she called it, art in this way. She said it was a sign of the world's decadence. She said she did not care for Pennell's pictures; they seemed to her a travesty, a caricature of art.

Carol's cheeks grew a shade pinker, and her eyes brighter. The neighbor on her left had finished his story and was hastily swallowing his ice, and she had an instant to herself. Almost she interrupted the conversation across the table, so eager was she to make that woman understand how those noble pictures had thrilled her, and how glad she was to see that common labor was at last glorified; a thing to contemplate and enjoy, not an ugly eyesore, a necessary evil that commerce might go on.

It was just at that moment that the hush came, and turning she saw that Fawcett at her side was standing. To her horror he was introducing her as the first speaker, the guest of honor who was to start the ball rolling.

Cold horror grappled at her throat, a great blinding wave seemed about to engulf her, the challenge of the universe against her soul confronted her. Somehow she got to her feet. Her face was still vivid and eager from her thoughts. Amid the storm of applause that followed her introduction she groped about in her mind for something to say. She caught at the little old joke she had memorized. It seemed a sickly straw to rest her weight upon, but she told it, amid a hush of interest that she attributed wholly to her Paris frock.

But amazing thing! The joke got across! Laughter bubbled up spontaneously, and applause floated out like a beautiful banner! But what should she say next? Her mind was a blank.

She waited while they laughed and applauded. The quiet smile that had been on her lips when she arose had not had wits to take itself away. It gave no hint of the tumult in her soul. She looked wide-eyed about the table, and across to the elderly cousin. Suddenly she knew that there was something she wanted to say to that woman, and there were no other things within her grasp. And because the silence had become tense and she must say something she began to describe one of Pennell's pictures that had impressed her mightily.

The subject was one of New York's great towering buildings in the making, the steel skeleton nearly completed, clear-cut against a stormy sky where clouds and blended smoke softened the harsh outlines of warehouses, and distance gave a hint of dome and tower and spire. Like a human spider on a network of steel cables a single being clung, doing some tiny part of the labor on the great structure. Strung far above the world at a dizzying height, where one mismove would hurl him to his death, he worked, nor seemed to know that heaven above and earth beneath were terribly far away.

As Carol described this picture in its clear bold outlines, the beauty of the noble structure and the beauty of the laborer who toiled suspended above daily peril were blended into one before their eyes, expressing together the very spirit of the steel. She felt suddenly that she had her audience in her spell.

Across the table the elderly cousin was leaning forward as if she had gained a new vision. The man with whom she had been talking listened eagerly as one who finds himself nobler than he knew, and every face was turned toward her with interest. Here was something out of the ordinary! This was no after-dinner speech. This was unique, original! Why, the girl was idealizing industry, putting it on a par with the arts. She seemed to be something of a genius!

All down the table coffee cups were forgotten, ices melted, while all eyes were turned to listen to the slender girl in her misty green frock with her red-gold hair and her sweet air of seriousness. Even Schlessinger and Blintz had lost their grins, and were listening in wonder.

Across from them the dark head of the young man was lifted, his fine eyes watching her intently. Something sparkled behind the question in his eyes. Was it sympathy? Surprise? Or perhaps a faint mistrust?

As she stopped to take breath she saw all this, and in a sudden wonder at it asked herself how she had done it and what she should say next? Her mind seemed just as blank for an instant as when she had begun. What scorn they would all feel if she broke down!

She swept them another glance as they still watched her gravely, eagerly, respectfully, and suddenly the thrill of their attention took hold of her once more, and she opened her lips again. Some of the things she said were what she had planned for Frederick Fawcett to say, and some had been seething in her brain all the way from home. She had meant to deal them out to the erring Duskin. But others were thoughts that had never to her knowledge been in her mind before, and as she gave them voice she wondered. It did not seem herself that was talking at all. And when she sat down amid profound applause she found herself weak with sudden fright, and wholly unable to account for the effect she had attained.

"That was great!" whispered Frederick Fawcett. "You put us across in great shape. It couldn't have been better!"

And while he rose to introduce the next speaker, the noted financier across the table bent his venerable silver head and gave her gallant compliment. But Carol scarcely heard what he said, so hard was she striving to control the trembling of her lips, the tendency of her throat to either cry or laugh hysterically.

When she got the better of herself again and looked up, the distinguished looking young man at the other end of the table was speaking. He was looking straight at her. His eyes were most penetrative. She almost felt that he was talking to her personally. She wished she knew who he was. She had not heard his name this time either. She wished she had listened. He seemed a strong character.

Then, suddenly he was done. She saw him look at his watch, rise, and nod farewell to the young woman who had sat next to him, and he was gone.

She found herself disappointed, as if the evening had suddenly gone flat. Searching her heart while others were making brief speeches mainly composed of stale jokes, she realized that she had wanted that man to stay long enough for her to find out if he too had approved of what she said. He had watched her with apparent interest but she was not sure that the later impression had eradicated his first one. She had wanted to know, and now she never would!

A great many people said a great many nice things to her. She could see that Mr. Fawcett was highly pleased, and that some of the men whom he had pointed out as important were much impressed by what she had said. But afterward when she thought over the evening she found it was only a blur of confusion upon which that one young man's strong face, and keen searching eyes stood out and looked at her. She felt as if he knew that she was only masquerading.

But the last thought before she slept was of the two men, Schlessinger and Blintz. What had become of them, and where would she meet them next?

Chapter 5

Morning brought elation, and a sense of triumph as she gradually recalled faces and expressions that showed she had succeeded in what she came to do. After all that was the important thing. If she could show her employer that she was capable of helping to pull the company out of this temporary embarrassment, surely it ought to be worth a raise in her salary.

But beyond that, even if that were not the result, she felt a satisfaction that she had made good. That she had been able to step into the real business world with men whose names were known the country over and hold her own. Of course in calm reflection, she realized that she had not said anything really important that she had not heard from Caleb Fawcett over and over again as she sat clicking her noiseless typewriter in her inner office, while conversations went on outside. The only thing that she had done that was worthwhile was to get their attention for a few facts by describing that picture she had seen in Washington. If it had not been for that beginning she might never have got her facts across to those hardheaded businessmen. And that beginning had come like an inspiration. She could not really take any credit for that.

Taking it all in all, Carol Berkley was rather humbled than otherwise by her triumph of the night before. She was born and brought up an honest girl, and she knew that no native brilliance of her own had made her speech such a success. Nevertheless when she went down later to meet Frederick Fawcett and receive anew his congratulations, she was feeling that now the hardest part of her work was done. If she could meet with the rich and great and not be overwhelmed surely she ought to find it easy to vanquish a mere upstart just out of college who was too much engaged in amusing himself coming up to Chicago, to get down to work and finish his job on time.

Fawcett showed her a copy of the telegram he had just sent off to his uncle in which her appearance the night before at the dinner was spoken of in highest praise. It could not but be gratifying to her to know that her employer, as well as the office at home, would know of her triumphs.

Fawcett insisted that she should stay over until the noon train and see a bit of Chicago. He took her for a drive along the north shore and gave her a glimpse in passing of the notable places, promising if she would come up again some weekend when his wife got home that they would be delighted to entertain her.

Altogether she was well pleased with her trip so far. Fawcett finally seated her in the parlor car of a local train, and she started on her way once more.

She spent the first half hour of her journey writing a letter to her mother, and then settled down to the contents of her briefcase. At the last minute before she started from the office at home she had taken from the file all correspondence with regard to the Duskin job, and now she took it out and began to go over it carefully. It would not do to go to Duskin without being thoroughly conversant with the whole situation. She thought she remembered everything pretty well, but she was taking no chance. She must have every little detail at her fingers' ends. There was no doubt in her mind but that she had slippery men to deal with, and from what those two men, themselves crooked as could be, had said of this Duskin, it would appear that he was the slipperiest of them all.

She opened the first letters and began to read. Here were Duskin's credentials. She had not seen them before. Duskin had undertaken the work before she had been promoted to Mr.

Fawcett's private office. They were almost extravagant in their praise. She curled an unbelieving lip. How people lied sometimes in writing letters of recommendation, or else in some cases, how they were deceived in the person they were recommending!

Here for instance was this Duskin. One of the letters said—it was from his college president—"I know of no more honorable, conscientious, energetic, promising young man in the whole of my acquaintance than Philip Duskin—" and another, this from the great head of an engineering firm with whom it appeared he had been connected for four years following his college experience, "This young man will accomplish any purpose he undertakes if it is humanly possible to accomplish."

How could those words be reconciled with the revealing words she had copied down in her office from the conversation of those two crooks? Of course they were *crooks* themselves, but they were not talking for other ears, and naturally what they told one another in privacy must be true. It certainly had sounded as if that young Duskin had joined with them in a scheme to substitute papier-mâché frescoes for the ceilings in place of the carvings which the contract called for. Blintz had even stated the sum they would thus be able to divide between the three of them. They had implied that Duskin had refused to be a party to the graft unless he shared equally in the booty. They had spoken of other materials where similar propositions had been made to Duskin, and where he had apparently acquiesced. Yet he had succeeded in deceiving his college president and his former employers so that they gave him recommendations like that! Oh, it would be a work of righteousness to expose him to the light of day! A young man ought to suffer for a deceit like that. He deserved to be in jail more than any common thief who stole a few dollars from somebody's purse.

And what of the two men who were supposed to be building

that structure? What could possibly be their object? It put an entirely new angle on the matter to find that they were the actual owners of the building. She had not had time last night after discovering their identity to think about it. She had been too weary when the evening was over, and the morning had been full of other things. There was something strange about it all which she felt she must ferret out. How could they be the owners of that building and yet be working a graft game on it? It did not seem reasonable that it was all explainable on the grounds that they wanted to make the Fawcett people lose their big forfeit. Of course, that would be a way to get their building at little cost, but what would they have when they were done? And would men really descend to a thing like that? And then plan to cheat themselves on the ceiling? It was most perplexing and she was satisfied that there was some key to it all that she did not yet understand. She must work it out slowly. She must not make a false move, nor show her hand on any account. Perhaps if she could get rid of this Duskin quietly and put another man in his place things would go through all right, and yet—where was she to get the other man? She had asked a few cautious questions of Frederick Fawcett, and he had said that there were comparatively few men well equipped and trustworthy, who were available at present for new jobs. Of course there were new untried ones, but one didn't dare put a new man on a big job, and if they were going to broaden out along the lines suggested at the banquet last night they would need to be looking around for good men and training them in readiness when the need arose.

She had not hinted that she might be in immediate need of one, but she had taken the precaution to jot down the name of the one man whom Fawcett mentioned as being the only one he knew at the present time who could be got in a hurry, and he was going up to Maine fishing. Ah! It might be that Maine would have yet to yield up another vacationer before many days!

She went on reading the letters, searching for the one she remembered. The first one that had come under her observation had complained about the rivets not coming, and the other about the paint being stolen. They had impressed her at the time as being items too trivial for a grown man to whine about. Now as she read the letter over again it did not seem quite so unbusinesslike as she had thought. The sentences were crisp, and to the point.

"The rivets we ordered from Cross and Keyes have not arrived. In consequence the work was held up a day or two. We were further delayed by the fact that a quantity of paint which had been locked in the office was stolen overnight, and no more of the right quality could be procured short of Chicago. I have put a double watch on the building now and hope to obviate further trouble, but these little holdups have been most unforeseen and unaccountable. We put the matter of the paint into the hands of the police who are trying to trace it, but Cross and Keyes have been unable as yet to get any clue to the lost rivets which they *say* they shipped immediately as agreed. Sometimes I feel that there is an enemy at work."

Of course that might be a mere amateurish way of making excuses to cover his own delinquencies. A young man who would go up to Chicago for a whole day and night and perhaps two days at this critical stage of the building game was likely too flighty to realize how inadequate he was to the situation.

Whatever became of those rivets anyway? There seemed to have been no further mention of them in the correspondence. Was he still sitting around waiting for the rivets to arrive? No wonder Mr. Fawcett was almost in a nervous breakdown over the situation. Why hadn't he fired that inefficient young man long ago? He ought to be writing fairy tales rather than business letters. It needed a man who could *do* things on a job like this. Well, she would see that things began to happen as soon as she got there anyway.

She looked impatiently out at the landscape. What a pity that she had to waste her time on this stupid stuff instead of having leisure to enjoy the new country through which she was passing. It was too bad. But she must get this case in hand. If only Mr. Fawcett would hurry up and get well and come and take the whole thing out of her hands! If only the speech and the last night's success could have been the end of her mission how pleasant it all would have been. Yet, she shrank from even those before she experienced them. Well, she would do the best she could, that was all that could be expected of her. Yet she knew in her heart that her whole interest was for the Fawcett Construction Company and she meant to see it win. She wanted to see those two contemptible crooks beaten—yes and the third young crook who had fallen apparently from the high estate where his friends seemed to think he belonged. She was out to win, and win she would if human effort could make that possible.

And then she wondered why that phrase sounded familiar just now, and was annoyed when she remembered it had been in one of Duskin's credentials.

When Carol finally reached her destination the first persons she saw as she stepped to the platform were Schlessinger and Blintz sitting in a great handsome car watching the stream of descending passengers. Quickly she dodged behind a tall man until she was safely inside the waiting room. Then she crossed to a door at the end and took a taxi. She told the driver she wanted to go to the best hotel, and she sat back out of sight and was whirled away down a noisy street and into traffic. Something told her those two men had been looking for her. Perhaps they were going to try to strike up a conversation. They might even approach her with their double-dealings. Her soul revolted at the thought. She remembered faintly the stories of her childhood. Was it the Little Red Hen that had such a time getting away from the fox? He put her in a big bag and carried her home to put in the pot of boiling water, only the Little Red Hen snipped a hole in the bag and rolled a big stone in her place and flew away. Well, she would bide her time till she was ready to snip a hole in any bag that they might try to put her in, and then she would run away and leave a big stone to splash them to disaster when they dropped it into the seething caldron of their own plots.

Carol got hastily through the preliminaries at the hotel. She had a haunting fear of seeing two men, one tall, one short and stout, arriving on the scene. They seemed to be peering at her from behind the desk, the fat upholstery, the heavy hangings of the great parlors.

She wrote her name quickly in small characters, C. W. Berkley Morningside. That would mean nothing to them she hoped even if they should examine the registry. She had not much hope of staying incognito for long, but perhaps she might get an opportunity to look over the situation before she had to face the old fox and begin the race.

She went straight to her room and erased the stains of travel, arranged for her trunk to be sent for, then picked up her Bible to snatch at another verse, feeling that somehow it might bring luck as it had the night before. But the first words her eyes fell upon were: "Be not wise in thine own eyes." It was like a dash of cold water on her growing pride. She shut the book hastily with a frown and went out to survey the land.

She knew from the papers she had brought where the building was located. She procured a map of the city and started out on foot. She wanted to get acquainted with the lay of the town before anyone knew she was there. She felt that unless she knew directions they could take great advantage of her.

When she turned into Maple Street from the roar and bustle of the main street, she sighted at once two buildings in process of construction, one a network of metal girders, the other standing solidly with walls of sturdy masonry. Her eyes turned at once toward the skeleton of steel. That of course would be hers. And the work had progressed no further than that! Her heart began to sink. Even her meager knowledge of construction told her that never in the world could she hope to rescue an operation from a preliminary state like that and get it finished and ready for occupancy in six weeks. Even six months would be inadequate to finish it from this mere outline. What could Mr. Fawcett have been thinking of that he did not find out sooner how the work had progressed? Surely someone was criminally at fault. And likely it was that man Duskin. Her heart sank for her employer. She saw that now unless a miracle happened the company was doomed. What ought she do? Telegraph for someone of the men from the office? There wasn't one who would know what to do in an emergency like this. Mr. Edgar Fawcett was the only one who could act with power. Something radical would have to be done, and done quickly. She didn't know what it would be. Ought she to send for Frederick Fawcett? Was he enough in the company's confidence to let him in on this tragedy that was hanging imminent over their heads, even while they were gaily planning for greater things and prating of expansion.

As she put these questions to herself she drew nearer, and stood looking up at the big openwork of the frame. It was half past three and workmen were still crawling like human spiders over the threadlike girders, tapping away on the rivets till the reverberations were like a great orchestra getting in tune.

What use to make a show of hurry like this when the time was almost up? They could not possibly finish now, why try at all? The forfeit was so great that disaster would be the only result.

Desolately, as if she herself were stricken, idly as if it did not matter what she did or where she went, now that she saw she had been championing a lost cause, she went across the street.

Chapter 6

She stood within the shadow of the sketchy structure, and looked up. The riveters were making a show of being hard at work. The rhythmic sound stuttered on and on, echoing melodiously, and the men seemed to be wasting no time. There was one tiny figure away up high watching them, doing nothing himself but smoking a cigarette. That would likely be Duskin, if he was even there at all. He must have just got back, had perhaps come on the same train she did. He was dressed too well to be standing up there in that dirt watching other men slave. He should have pulled off his coat and taken a hand. But then he likely didn't know how. He was paid for watching the others. She curled her lip disdainfully.

It was a dizzying business looking up so high, and the sun shining straight in her eyes. Dust was sifting down too. She stopped looking up and glanced around.

There was a wooden shed over the sidewalk, and foot passengers had to step out in the street to get around it. There was an opening near where she stood, and Carol in spite of a great sign "NO ADMITTANCE!" stepped within. If she had to get at this business she might as well begin at once. Working hours would be over in a little while, and then she would have to wait for a new day. She must find Duskin at once and get rid of him. Certainly that must be the first step. Then she would go and call Chicago on the telephone and get in touch with the other man, what was his name, Delaplaine? Edgar Delaplaine. She would tell him he must come down on the night train and be ready to take charge in the morning.

With that she came face to face with a burly laborer who carried a great load of rivets on his shoulders. He was on his way to the rude stair that led up airily above her head.

"Nobody allowed in here, Miss," said the laborer gruffly. "Better git out fore the boss sees you. He call the police onto the las' one cum inside. Can't you all read? Didn' you all see the sign 'no 'd'mittance' ?"

"I am looking for Mr. Duskin," said Carol with dignity, trying to show that she had a right there.

"Who'm?" frowned the laborer. "Ain't no Duskin round these diggin's. Don' make no difference no how. Ladies ain't 'lowed to come see the laborers. Better git out."

"I wish to see the manager," said Carol drawing herself up haughtily now, "I represent the New York office."

"Can't help who you represents," persisted the man, edging her along toward the opening. "Ain't no 'd'mittance in here. Boss said so!"

"But I wish to *see* the boss," said Carol desperately.

"Boss gone to Chicago. Havta wait till t'morra, mebbe next day. Boss won't see nobody in here anyhow. Havta go to that office door down on Ellum street. Try him day after t'morra, lady, but you gotta git outta here now."

"For pity's sake!" exclaimed Carol. "Hasn't he come back yet? That's the limit! How long has he been gone?"

A big red-haired Irishman appeared on the scene.

"Hey, what's holdin' you up, Sam. Bony up there's sore's a pup 'cause you don't bring them rivets."

He leveled hard eyes on the shrinking girl who tried to draw her slipping cloak of dignity about her.

"I represent the New York office. I wish to see Mr. Duskin," she said haughtily, although she was ready to cry with impatience.

"Who? Duskin? We ain't got no such—Wait! You want Duskin? You're on the wrong job. We ain't got no New York office."

He led the reluctant Carol outside the board shelter and pointed to the end of a great gray stone building towering solidly up to heaven. She looked, and blinked at the bright sunlight, and tried to count the stories. Then because the red-haired Irishman had planted himself firmly behind her and across the opening of the board shelter where she had just been, and she could not feel it would be of any use to try to get back there just now, she started up the street. The man was wrong of course. But at least she might be able to find someone in the other building to direct her, or someone who would send word to Duskin or whoever he had left in charge while he played around in Chicago.

But when she came opposite the great stone structure she was suddenly confronted by a large sign across its front bearing in black letters the startling words:

FAWCETT CONSTRUCTION COMPANY

She paused in amazement, almost coupled with annoyance. She had been wrong, all wrong, right at the start! The red-haired man had been right! And she had intruded where she had no right! A sudden desire came over her to sit down on the stone steps, and rest her weary overstrained body, and laugh aloud. But she reflected that that would be no way in which to meet the erring Duskin in case he should chance to take it into his head to return to his job. She must pull herself together and do something sensible. She felt as if all the men in both buildings were watching her and making fun of her.

She walked slowly up the street till she came to a drugstore. She went in and ordered an orange soda. She felt very foolish and humbled. How silly of her not to have looked for a sign, or asked someone before she went into that place. She must learn to be less impulsive. She was no businesswoman yet, even if she had made a speech that pleased a few rich businessmen.

The words of the Bible verse she had just read kept coming back to her like a taunt, a warning, and brought a mortified color to her cheeks: "Be not wise in thine own eyes." Never again would she say Proverbs was impersonal.

More soberly now she went back to the big gray stone building and went up the steps.

The door stood open and a man was mixing paint in the back end of the long hall. There was a pleasant smell of new plaster in the air, and there was heavy building paper fastened securely over the floors covering the tiles beneath. She knew they were tiles by the way they felt as she stepped over the paper, and because the paper was torn away in one corner disclosing the tesselated floor of clear black and white marble.

She walked the length of the hall, taking in everything, the lofty well proportioned rooms, the staircase also done in paper, the smooth walls seemingly all ready for their decoration, the electric wires hanging through holes in the ceiling and walls at frequent intervals. Why, the place seemed almost finished! This could not be the building. She must have made a mistake again.

She picked her way past the open elevator shafts, between kegs of nails and cans of paint, and spoke to the man who continued to mix paint as if his life depended on it.

"Is this the Fawcett Construction Company operation?" she asked, clearing her throat of a sudden huskiness. Her voice echoed weirdly and was flung back to her in volumes from the height of unseen corridors.

"Yep," said the man without pausing in his mixing, but lifting a mildly approving eye to her trim little figure.

"Well, can you tell me when they expect Mr. Duskin back?"

" 'Uskin 'ack!" echoed her voice from seemingly miles away like an angry witch that inhabited the air above her.

"Back?" said the man lifting his head now and giving her an appraising eye. "He got back las' night. Been workin' most all night by hisself to ketch up. Never did see sech a man. Come back in his sleep ef he couldn't get here no other way!" The man continued to mix rhythmically.

Carol surveyed him coldly. She was not sure but he was trying to joke about it. She was no longer in a laughing mood. This was serious business. She must send some sort of a telegram to the hospital to Fawcett tonight, something the doctor would consider encouraging, and here it was almost quitting time.

"Where—could I see him?" she asked hesitantly. "When?"

"Right now!" responded the man with alacrity, "He's up on the 'leventh. Wait! I'll have ye hauled up!"

He gave five more distinct stirs to his paint before he lifted the stick with which he stirred it, scraped it off neatly on the edge of the can, and rose from his stooping posture.

Carol looked around wildly wondering what the process of being hauled up would entail.

The man went to the edge of the elevator shaft and looked up:

"Hoooo! Bill! Send down that shutter! Passenger wantsta come up!"

A voice came fluttering down from above like a piece of paper that whirled around at every draft.

"Ooo! Ay! Awwright!"

And presently there appeared in midair a man's legs standing on a slender raft and then the whole man airily descending holding a heavy rope in his hand.

The raft arrived and the man eyed her disapprovingly.

"Step aboard!" said the painter. "She wantsta see the boss, Bill!" Bill eyed the lady disapprovingly:

"The boss won't talk now. He's awful busy. He said he wouldn't have no reporters on the job, Dan."

Carol stepped aboard quickly.

"I'm not a reporter," she said briskly. "I've come from Mr. Fawcett in New York with a message. Take me up, please."

Bill surveyed her with alien eyes:

"The boss is awful busy now. You'd best lemme tell him yer here. They've set to git the wiring on the 'leventh done t'night. A salesman was just here, and the boss almost fired him down the shaft he was that mad!"

"Take me up!" said Carol crisply with command in her eye. "He won't fire *me* down the shaft!"

So that was what Duskin was up to. Somehow he had found out she was coming. Likely Frederick Fawcett had let it out yesterday that he had had word from the office or something, and Duskin was putting up a big bluff of working hard. But he couldn't deceive her. She knew too much.

As the big rope in the man's hand slid the frail raft up and up inch by inch Carol was planning a dramatic arrival.

As floor after floor slid slowly by, she was interested in spite of herself to see the progress that had been made. Why, to her inexperienced eyes it did not look after all as if there was so much to be done. And yet, the letters had been constantly prating of setbacks as if they were a weekly menace. Well, there was surely some crooked game being played here. She must keep her eyes open wide and her mouth shut, and she must be careful not to let anyone know how much she knew until she was good and ready to make her revelation.

The raft came to an unsteady stop at last, and Carol had a flashing view of the depths below, eleven stories down and then basements and cellars beneath. She caught her breath as she stepped quickly off and looked about her.

"Boss is in there," said Bill with an inscrutable look in his eye and a sound in his voice as if he were discreetly anticipating something.

Carol stepped to the doorway of a large bright room and saw three men in overalls hard at work, one working at the far end of the room by a window screwing something into a hole in the wall, one on a ladder pulling a heavy wire tube up through another hole in the wall, and the third down on the floor over a ripped up board with a pair of pliers in his hand, watching the other end of the wire cable move along in the open space.

The moment seemed tense. No one noticed her arrival, although her steps along the corridor had been brisk and business-like. She paused in the doorway and studied each man, waiting an instant for someone to look up.

But no one looked up. Each man was intent upon his particular job. From the floor below there came the rhythmic sound of a saw seething through wood and driven by a master hand. Hammer blows mingled with cheery whistling. Perhaps they had not heard her.

"Can you tell me where to find Mr. Duskin?" Carol's voice was clear and sailed around the empty room resonantly. There could be no doubt but that they had heard her speak, but not a man of the three stirred or even lifted an eyelash. Were they all deaf-mutes?

She stepped a foot nearer to the man on the floor and repeated her question.

"Easy, easy there, Charlie, she's coming slack. Just an inch more—there! Now hold her!" The pliers went into the dark notch in the floor and did something, but still no man of the three paid the slightest heed to her.

She glanced about and there in the doorway stood the man Bill, a wicked twinkle in his eyes, licking his lips with anticipation, but he did not move or make the slightest suggestion of coming to her rescue. She thought he rather enjoyed her discomfiture.

She stood, wondering just how to make her next attack. Then the man on the floor spoke again, his eyes still on the thing in the floor that his pliers held:

"Now, Charlie, hold her. She's all right!"

An instant's more silence during which Carol at last seemed to sense that there was something important going on that she must not interrupt and then the man on the floor dropped his pliers by the hole and rose to his feet facing about to meet her astonished gaze. Of all things! The man in overalls was that distinguished looking young man whom she had met at the dinner last night! What on earth could he be doing here? Perplexities were thickening. She experienced a sudden wild wish that she had never heard of Fawcett and Company and that she were at that instant sitting on the sand in Maine watching the quiet waves creep up on the shore.

The young man's eyes were grave and piercing. His look was like the one he had given her last night when he turned away after she had told Schlessinger she would fire Duskin. Was he then a friend of Duskin's. Did that explain his look? He was perhaps some college friend working for an experience perchance that he might write a book about it afterwards.

"I beg your pardon," she managed to say, suddenly realizing that she had been introduced to him the night before, and must not treat him like a stranger or a common workingman, "I am looking for Mr. Duskin. Can you tell me where to find him?"

A flash of surprise went across the keen gray eyes, and he looked at her steadily, then spoke almost curtly:

"I am Duskin." He did not take his eyes from her face. It seemed that he was sifting her down to her thoughts. She had a feeling that there would not be anything hid from him if he undertook to find it out.

"*You* are Mr. Duskin?" she said in great astonishment, and then tried to gather her scattered senses. Of course she must not let him see that she was utterly flabbergasted by this. It would be disastrous to do that.

"I'm afraid I did not understand the name last night," she managed sweetly with a frigid little smile. In spite of herself she could not help feeling more friendly to him. So this was how he had managed to get the job. He had a personality that took people. Poor Mr. Fawcett had been taken by his looks, and so had that college president and all those others who had recommended him. And he was trying those fine eyes on her now. He knew by her speech last night that she had come down to look after the interests of the company, and he was going to forestall anything she might be going to say. He wouldn't be so sure of himself of course when he read Mr. Fawcett's peevish letter. But she must be on her guard. He certainly could appear to be something quite unusual, even in these workmen's overalls. Of course that was a pose. A dramatic touch to show her how hard he was working!

These thoughts raced through her brain as she took out the letter from her handbag and presented it:

"Mr. Duskin, I have here a letter for you from Mr. Fawcett. Perhaps you would like to read it before I say anything further."

Without a change of countenance, or a lifting of those eyes from her face, Duskin took the letter and stuffed it into the pocket of his overalls.

"All right," he said, "I'll try to get time to read it sometime tonight. You'll excuse me now. I've got to get back to work. The men who started to wire this place made some bad blunders that wouldn't pass inspection. The inspector is coming again early tomorrow morning and every wire on half the floors has got to be changed to comply with the law. I went up to Chicago yesterday to get a new set of men, and we shall have to work all night to get it done. We've had all kinds of a time getting the inspector to come and he's promised he won't fail us, and we've got to be ready. Sorry to seem discourteous but this can't be helped. Bill, you'd better take the lady down. She will only be uncomfortable up here."

Carol's cheeks flamed indignantly:

"But you don't understand," she protested, "I've come—"

"I understand perfectly, Miss Berkley. You've come to fire me, but unfortunately I haven't time to be fired now. I'll talk with you later. Bill, take Miss Berkley down, and if anybody else tries to come up, shoot them."

Carol stood in utter rout and saw her plans falling away from her like a house of cards. How was she to manage a man like this? Would she have to telephone for the police to get him off the job?

Then she heard a scraping, puffing noise in the hall and lifting her eyes she saw just beyond the elevator shaft where the open stairway showed, two men like two porpoises, a long one and a round one, snorting, panting up the stairs.

She turned one panic-stricken glance at Duskin and stepped into the frail raft beside Bill, the grinning Bill.

Chapter 7

In something like a panic of defeat Carol got herself back to the hotel and up to her room and locked the door.

As she snapped on the light she caught a glimpse of her Bible lying on the bureau, and a single sentence began to ring in her ears, over and over, "Be not wise in thine own eyes! Be not wise in thine own eyes!" until her cheeks began to burn.

She sat down to think what she should do next, but instead she broke down and cried. Just why she was crying she did not know. Was it because that man had been rude to her again? Was it because she had failed to fire him in the final and brief manner she had planned? Was it because Fawcett and Company were in such a hole and she couldn't see any way to get them out? Or was it because those two horrid men kept coming into the scene and filling her with disgust?

She did not know. She only knew she was tired to a frazzle, and sick of the whole thing, and she would like to go home and cry in her mother's arms the way she used to do when she was a little girl.

And she wasn't being the grand and glorious success in the business world at all as they had made her think last night. She was just a silly little secretary who was trying to do a man's job and failing. Failing at every turn, and getting snubbed and turned down. Look how they had put her out of that other operation! Of course a man would have known better than to get himself into the wrong building. A man would have informed himself beforehand. A man would have known by instinct without even asking anyone where the right place was.

And then look how that Duskin creature had treated her! As if she were the offscouring of the earth! How unspeakably rude he was! And thought he could get away with it just because he had fine eyes! Well, he would find he couldn't with her! She might have been upset by his first onslaught but she wouldn't be again. She would be ready for him. She would think out a campaign fully. Which she should have done, of course, before she arrived here. But how could she when she didn't know what she was up against? But now she would be prepared. She would have no mercy on him. He was quite impossible! She had meant to give him one more chance if he seemed at all amenable, but it was plain that there was absolutely no hope of him. He was the kind of man who would do nothing but his own way, and well she knew what Mr. Fawcett thought of that! She had been sent on here to put a stop to that. But she would get ready. There was a way to deal with everyone, and she would deal most summarily with him.

"Be not wise in thine own eyes," chanted that verse again. She wished she had never seen it.

Of course, she should really have stayed and done it at once. But how could she deal with Mr. Duskin while Schlessinger and Blintz stood by and grinned. That was quite impossible in spite of her gay boast to them last night. Besides it was not the dignified thing to dismiss a manager while anyone else was listening. She would make it quite plain to Duskin in the morning—she must by all means see him in the morning—that that was the *only* reason why she had not been final with him this afternoon: she did not wish to humiliate him before others.

Having settled so much in her mind she threw her weary young body down upon the bed, and arranged herself comfortably to think out her campaign.

The pillows were downy, the box springs and mattress were all that is perfect in a bed, and the girl was very weary. Just to rest her eyes she closed them for a moment, and before she had decided whether to call in the police to aid her in the morning, or to call up Delaplaine that night on long distance and have him on hand for the interview with Duskin, she had dropped fast asleep.

Sometime in the night she awoke with a start and found she was cold, and the room was absolutely dark. The stir of the city had gone dead and the blackness of night was about her.

Searching about for the light she snapped it on and looked at her watch. It was two o'clock, and she was drowned in sleep! It was no use trying to work out a campaign until she got rested. She slipped off her dress and shoes, found her kimono and unceremoniously got into bed dropping straight off to sleep again, with only a passing indignant memory of hard, cold, fine eyes that defied her.

Duskin had remained standing exactly where she left him until the temporary elevator had descended out of sight. Then he turned his gaze toward the two men who had paused on the stairway three steps below the top to stare down toward the crazy lift. They were still puffing, and leaning over the elevator shaft which was just beside the stairway, their mouths open wonderingly, their brows drawn questioningly. Had they arrived too late?

"Oh, is that you, Blintz? Schlessinger? You better stop right where you are. We've got a lot of exposed wires around here and it isn't safe to monkey with them. I've just sent someone else down and told Bill not to let any more up till we get things fixed safe again."

Blintz drew back from the edge of the shaft sharply and let go of the wooden rail that had been nailed up temporarily until the fireproof wall should be finished.

"Live wires?" he questioned sharply, his apoplectic pink face blanching at the thought. "Hear that, Mr. Schlessinger? They've got live wires up there! We'd better go down. Is it all safe on the stairs, Duskin?"

"Just stand right where you are, Blintz. Nothing can harm you there. And when you hear the lift begin to come up you go down to the next floor and wait there. I'll send Bill to take you down. That's safer."

"But that's all nonsense, Duskin," put in Schlessinger. "Can't you tell us where to step? I've got to see you at once. It's something very important I must tell you. A tip you'll want to have."

Schlessinger started up another step. He was not so badly winded as his stouter brother.

"Stop right where you are, Schlessinger!" said Duskin with sharp command in his voice. "I'll not be responsible if you don't obey orders. Sorry, Mr. Schlessinger, but you'll have to let the tips go until another time."

Blintz by this time was padding down the steps rapidly, keeping carefully in the middle of the stairs. Schlessinger hesitated:

"Well, then, come downstairs for a minute. I tell you it's important."

"Can't possibly leave now," said Duskin impatiently. "The lift is coming back. You better hurry! Bill," he called down the shaft, "take these two men down and show them out past all open wires."

"All right, sir!" shouted Bill with a tone that had a grin in the end of it.

"But I must see you at once!" shouted Schlessinger as he turned slowly and went down the stairs.

"Call you up as soon as I can make it!" shouted Duskin cheerfully to the top of Schlessinger's head as it disappeared down below the edge of the elevator shaft. Then turning sharply around:

"Charlie, got that fastened? Good boy! Let's go to the next room, and, Ted, when Bill gets back tell him to lock that front door and not to let another fool in on his life! Get me?"

"Right, sir!" grinned Ted coming to life for the first time since Carol's appearance.

The afternoon wore away.

Half past four came and the carpenters on the tenth floor folded their aprons and locked their tool chests and filed downstairs. More carpenters came whistling down from the eleventh floor, paused to say good-night respectfully to the boss's back as they passed. Duskin answered with a cheery good-night, without stopping his work or turning his head.

The sun dropped lower and sent long shafts of red and amber across the walls where they worked, but still they went on with grim set faces. Six o'clock struck and a gang of five blue-eyed, sandy Scotchmen came up and looked gravely into the room which Duskin and his men had just reached in their round of the eleventh floor.

"We've done the tenth, Dusky," said one who seemed to be the boss of the crew. "We're goin' out to get a bite of grub and then we'll come back and tackle the ninth."

"Good work, Roddy!" said Duskin rising from the floor for a keen look at the men. "How'd you find it down there? Pretty rotten?"

"Worse'n rotten. A mess! If you was ta ask me I'd say those birds never touched a 'lectric wire before in their sweet lives. Didn't even know how ta fake it. Top floors are the worrrst. They didn't dare put over some of their trricks where they'd be noticed. Better stop an hour, Dusky, and come with us. You've been at it all day!"

"All day!" sneered Charlie. "Better say all night! He come up here straight from the midnight owl train and never went out since. Had Bill bring him up some coffee and a sandwich at noon and that's all."

"Aw shut up, Charlie," said Duskin turning a weary smile on his assistant, "I'm no martyr. If I get this done in time for that inspector tomorrow morning I'll eat a meal that'll put you all in the shade. You forget I attended a banquet last night, worse luck. If I hadn't had to I'd have had more done before you all got here this morning."

"Aw, cut that out! We'll make it, Dusky!" said the blue-eyed one. "Come on out'n eat. There's a whole night before us ain't touched yet!"

Duskin turned sharply back to his wires.

"I'm not leaving this building till this wiring is done!" he said in the tone they all knew. "This happened when my back was turned, and I've got to camp on the job now till it's over. I can't run any more risks. Charlie, you and Ted and Pete go on with the rest. I'm staying here. You can bring me a snack when you come back but I'm staying here!"

"Come on then, boys! Don't let's waste time arguing," said Roddy. "Come on, Charlie!"

"You fellas go. I'm not leaving the boss alone in this shack," said Charlie. "There's liable to be enemies around! Ted, you and Pete go with Roddy's gang."

"We're waiting till Roddy gets back," said Ted doggedly, and went on twisting wires.

"What's the matter of Roddy bringing back enough for the gang?" said Pete. "I can't be bothered stopping. There's my thermos bottle over there. It'll hold three cups and Ted's got one."

"Okay," said Roddy cheerfully, picking up the bottles and departing.

"That's nonsense!" said Duskin sharply. "And anyhow Bill's here. Bill is staying here all the time now."

"Good boy! But Bill's only one. Can't tell how many little birdies might come round. Anyhow we're sticking. Ain't we, Ted?"

"Sure thing!" said Ted solemnly.

"You said it!" echoed Pete hauling a coil of insulated wire across to his location.

"Boys, I appreciate this," said Duskin gravely, "more than words can tell!"

"We ain't got done appreciatin' what you done for us over in France, Dusky," said Charlie in a very low tone and then immediately broke into boisterous song. From that the work went steadily on.

Forty minutes later Roddy's gang returned with steaming coffee in a big coffeepot, sandwiches, hot hard-boiled eggs and two big pies. The rest knocked off and made a hearty meal, encouraged thereto by the voices of song and whistling that came up the elevator shaft. They knew the other gang were doing the next floor.

Roddy slipped up to get some insulating tubes and volunteered a bit of comfort.

"Took a look on my way down, Dusky. Guess they didn't get to do much monkeying below the ninth. It may not take us so long after all."

"That's good!" said Duskin flashing a look of appreciation at him across the room. "Hope you're right!"

That was all that broke the monotony of tense steady labor until a little after midnight when Bill came up in the so-called elevator and brought a consignment of soup, rolls, and coffee with two custard pies. Roddy's gang came up and they had fifteen minutes of relaxation, where coffee and dry sayings were passed about liberally, and low contented laughter went around; they were all boys together. Duskin in overalls, drinking coffee out of a tin cup with the rest was as much at home here as he had been the evening before in the banquet hall in his dinner coat. If Carol could have seen him she would have been still more perplexed.

The last crumb of pie crust devoured, the last drop of coffee drained, and the gang departed to their various locations.

The night wore on. In her quiet hotel the weary representative of the Fawcett Construction Company lay in her soft bed and slept, and dreamed of how she would fire the boss the next day.

When morning dawned the men were still at work, drifting down to the lower floors, silently now, for there were footsteps along the early streets, and no whistling might come from the big unfinished building for chance workmen to hear and gossip about.

The men bore no sign of their night's vigil, but the light of victory in their eyes. But the boss turned a white face toward them all at last. There were dark circles under his eyes, the eyes that carried the light of another hindrance overcome, another difficulty surmounted, as he said:

"Well, fellows, we've done it! You've helped me to beat the dirty crooks again. I couldn't have put it across without you. Now beat it over to the hotel. Get a wash and a meal and then sleep all day. I'll see you at half past four if it's possible, and we'll plan what next. You've put real heart into me."

They hesitated as they turned toward the lift. Said Charlie:

"What about the dame? Anything to her chatter?"

A shadow flitted across the tired face of the boss.

"No, Charlie, just another small explosion. It's annoying, but this too shall pass!" he ended with a grin. "I'll settle her when I get time. She really doesn't know what she's talking about, you know."

So they passed out into the sunlight and Duskin went to a little corner in the cellar to wash his face, and take on the similitude of a manager before the morning arrival of the carpenter gangs. No one must suspect that the work had been going on all night.

Carol was awakened by the ringing of the telephone close to her ear. For a moment she thought she was back home in the office, and reached out in what she thought was the direction of her desk telephone. But her hand coming in sharp contact with the headboard of her bed brought her to her senses, and she sat up and looked around her.

Perceiving that it was morning and her room phone was ringing she answered it, conscious of quick alarm. If Duskin had come to talk with her what should she say? She had fallen asleep before she had decided anything.

She answered the telephone tremulously, "Yes?"

"Mr. Schlessinger is calling to see Miss Berkley," came the voice over the wire.

Panic clutched at her heart. Schlessinger again! What should she do? How had he found out where she was? Wasn't there any way at all of getting away from those two men?

She hesitated so long that the clerk in the office gave the message over again,

"Mr. Schlessinger wishes to see Miss Berkley as soon as convenient."

Carol spoke. She was surprised that her voice sounded cool and even:

"It will be impossible for me to see anyone this morning. I have some writing to do which must get off in the first mail, and a conference following. Say to Mr. Schlessinger that I will not be at liberty until," she paused wildly trying to think some way out of the situation, "at least until five o'clock," she finished desperately, and wondered how she was going to work her program out to fit this.

But the voice on the wire was persistent:

"Mr. Schlessinger wishes to speak to you."

Carol drew a quick breath of excitement. She would not talk to that man. Not now anyway.

"I have no time just now. Mr. Schlessinger will have to excuse me. I must go at once or I will be too late with my appointment." She hung up the receiver and looked about the room guiltily as though she expected the old fox to send up a search warrant for her arrest.

"Now," she said to herself, "I shall have to do something at once. I shall have to make some plan! I simply can't meet that man until I have some definite way out of this thing. I know he is going to try to worm something out of me that ought not to be told, and I'm afraid he will put me into a corner where my very silence will tell what I would rather die than breathe. He is like that I'm sure. He has no limitations, no refinements!"

She sprang out of bed and dressed as rapidly as possible in a becoming little sports dress of a new shade of blue called mountain mist. It had been designed for morning wear on the beach, and she sighed as she drew the blouse over her head, and adjusted the well hanging pleats of the stylish little skirt. It certainly was becoming. But why should it be wasted in this far alien town? She had no desire to be dressed becomingly for Schlessinger and Blintz, much less for that young man with steel swords in his eyes who refused to recognize her authority. Of course she hadn't wanted to take this position and wield authority over anyone, but being there by necessity she meant to be obeyed.

She shut her lips tight as she arranged the red-gold waves of her shining hair. She meant to do things today that would count. She was thoroughly rested and entirely herself again. This was a part of her job, and she would do it. That young man would see that he had met his master!

And a very firm little person she looked to be as she took her seat beside the telephone stand and called for long distance. She had decided that the thing to do was to get this Delaplaine on the wire and hire him to come at once, and then to send for Duskin.

As she waited for her call to go through, it occurred to her that Duskin might refuse to come to a conference; very likely he would. In which case she would wait for Delaplaine and take him with her to Duskin, get a policeman to go along if necessary, and put Duskin off the property. She felt that she ought to be prepared to go to all lengths with a man who she was practically sure was a crook. He had to understand that her word was law!

While she was still waiting for her call to go through, the office clerk asked again if Miss Berkley would speak to Mr. Schlessinger, about something very important, but Carol cut the idea short by saying she had a long distance call in and could not risk delaying it. She added that Mr. Schlessinger might send up a note if the matter was so important, but the clerk said that Mr. Schlessinger did not care to write what he had to say and would return again in an hour and hope to see her.

Panic took hold of Carol. She must be out of here in an hour unless she was willing to talk to Schlessinger, and as she felt now she would never be willing to talk to him. She had been rereading the notes she had taken of the talk she had overheard between him and his partner in crime, and the more she thought about it in the light of what had already been revealed, the more she felt that she did not want to trust herself to say anything to him. Indeed she wanted nothing at all to do with him.

She paced the floor in her agitation and watched the hands of her little wristwatch anxiously. She had put on her hat and had her gloves and handbag ready to go out. She planned to slip down the stairs rather than take the elevator, and slide out some side entrance and take a cab. In that way she might escape Schlessinger. She felt terribly alone. She almost contemplated telegraphing for her mother, or even Betty, in her desperation.

While she waited she opened her Bible to get that item out of her day and reading on down the chapter she lighted on these words: "The Lord shall be thy confidence, and shall keep thy foot from being taken."

It was almost uncanny. Perhaps she was getting superstitious. Certainly she would never say again that Proverbs was impersonal!

Then at last the call came from Chicago. But it was only to say that Mr. Delaplaine was out of town. He might be at home sometime during the day but it was doubtful. He had gone on a motor trip.

What right had a man in a business life to go off on a motor trip when he might be wanted? she asked herself bitterly. The voice went on to say that Mr. Delaplaine's mother was there. Would she talk with her, or leave a message?

Carol decided to leave a message for Delaplaine to call her up at once as soon as he came home, that he was wanted to take charge of a job at the earliest possible moment. Then, as she noted that the hour was nearly up, she picked up gloves and bag, locked her room door and fled the hotel.

Her meanderings through the halls and down various staircases brought her out at last at a side door which also connected with the tearoom and grill, but though she was hungry, seeing she had had no dinner the night before, and had been too late and too busy to order breakfast sent up to her room, she dared not risk going in lest Schlessinger might have her paged, and somehow ferret her out and come to sit with her.

There was no taxi in sight at the moment she emerged from the hotel, so she crossed the street and went around a corner quickly to a small side street, crossed again, and so winding about, she came to a small neat looking cafeteria and here she dared to take refuge. There were few people at that hour, and she took a seat far back in the room where she would not be noticed from the street, and turned her face away from the door.

The coffee was good and the rolls and eggs that she ordered were hot and fresh. She came away feeling quite refreshed both in mind and body. At least she had escaped those haunting men for a while. She would go and sit in a little park that she saw a block further on. It seemed to be a quiet, domestic neighborhood, hardly the spot she would expect to find either Schlessinger or Blintz at this hour of the morning. She sought out a seat behind a group of shrubs where she was well hidden from the street and sat down.

Her mind was in a tumult. She did not know what to do. She must not waste time like this, but she seemed balked at every turn. If only Mr. Fawcett were well enough she would telephone to him and ask his advice. But after what the doctor had said that was not to be thought of.

Five minutes of retirement behind the park shrubs put her nearly frantic. She realized that at any minute there might come a long distance from Delaplaine. Also, she might be missing a call from Duskin, although she felt very uncertain whether he would come near her if she waited six months for him.

At last she decided to call up the hotel and see if anything had happened.

She crossed the park to a small drugstore where she saw a telephone sign, and called her hotel.

No, there had been no call from Chicago. No long-distance call at all. Yes, Mr. Schlessinger had been there and waited for some time. He had just gone. He had said he would telephone later to see if she was back. No, there was no mail, but a note had come by special messenger. They had put it in her box. No, it could not have been from Mr. Schlessinger; it came while he was still there waiting for her.

Chapter 8

Carol came out of the telephone booth and took a taxi back to the hotel. It was a quarter to twelve and she had to know what that note contained.

When she reached the hotel she went in the side entrance and walked up the stairs. She would not risk meeting Schlessinger. In her room she telephoned down for her mail to be sent up to her.

The note was from Duskin. How had he found her address? Did everybody in this miserable little town know everything that went on? How had Schlessinger found out where she was staying?

The note simply said:

> Will you lunch with me at the University Club at one-thirty sharp? I will look for you in the small reception room to the right as you enter. Am much rushed for time, but there is a quiet table there where we can talk while we eat.
>
> Hastily,
> PHILIP DUSKIN.

The angry color rolled into her cheeks as she read. And he thought he could get by by inviting her to lunch! The impertinence of him! The audacity! Insult her and then invite her to lunch with him!

She wouldn't go of course, not a step. Why should he suppose that she wanted to talk with him? Suggesting a quiet place as if she would be willing to have a conference with him, after what he had said to her last night! It was preposterous!

And yet, as she pondered the matter, she realized that if she would talk with the man at all this was her only chance of contact. He had declined, and successfully, to talk with her on the job, had openly flouted her before the laborers. She had every reason to expect that he would do so again if she attempted to go there and tell him she was done with his services. It was all too evident that he did not recognize her right to give him orders or to dismiss him. She must show him her credentials, and there was no way to do that without meeting him. Of course, she could decline to eat when she got there. She could say she had already lunched, but would tell him what she had to say while he ate, if he was in such a grand hurry. He wouldn't be in a hurry anymore when she got through with him. His great rush would be over for this time at least, because there wouldn't be anything to hurry for! He would be out of a job. All the hurrying he would need to do after that would be to hustle for another job.

She shut her lips with satisfaction as she went about putting a few added touches to her already charming toilet. After all, one could talk better when one had the consciousness of being well dressed. She had learned that lesson from the little jade velvet.

As she adjusted the close white felt hat on her shining hair she reflected that she was dressed quite as appropriately now for lunching at an exclusive college club, as she had been the other night for banqueting with the great.

She dusted a small speck from her trim white slipper, picked up her white gloves, and white silk handbag from the bureau, and started out again on the warpath.

But her eyes were shining dangerously bright, and her cheeks needed no rouge to give them warm color. She was swallowing her pride and going to meet her man, but he would have to pay for it in the end. She was wearing her war paint now, and was in fine mettle. Thoughts came thick and fast of what she would tell him when she got him cornered as she knew she could. She had a few papers in her handbag which she would bring out, one at a time, at the proper moment, and one or two things to say, and if he enjoyed his lunch after that he was thicker skinned than even she had thought him.

The University Club building was quite imposing. She was impressed in spite of herself. She had not expected it in this small unimportant western town. "Back country town" she had called it in her metropolitan-trained mind.

He was not in sight when she entered the small reception room on the right where he had told her to wait for him. She frowned at the thought that he was going to keep her waiting, after daring to command her to be on time "sharp!" That was such an unpleasant word, as if she were a little school scholar and he her teacher. Stage stuff again, just to impress her of course! She half meditated slipping out again and keeping him waiting for her. She glanced at her watch. There were yet three seconds to the time, and even as she looked he stood beside her, courteous, quiet as any gentleman might be, as if he were the pleasant stranger she had thought him night before last when as strangers their eyes met across the room. She had a passing wish that it had been so, and that Duskin were another man, whom she did not know, and could never admire. Then she heard his voice:

"Shall we go right out to the dining room without wasting any more time?"

She arose hastily, remembering her anger, and all she had to say, and walked beside him the length of the beautiful hall with its glimpses of other reception rooms, furnished in rich taste, and of people here and there in pleasant groups. He was saying something about the house having been given by some famous millionaire in honor of his son who had been a university man, and she was following his words, and wondering at his manner. Could this be the same man she had seen in overalls lying on the floor with the pliers in his hand? In a tumult of soul she followed him to the table in a secluded nook by a window and sat down. Once more she had somehow lost the thread of what she had intended to say. She found the dignity and self-confidence that would have helped her to dominate him slipping slowly from her. There was something about this man that simply would not be dominated. And yet she must. She set her lips and resolved not to yield to the fascination.

There were flowers on the table, expensive hothouse roses of a delicate golden-hearted pink. A quick glance around showed her that theirs was the only table so decorated. Did that mean that Duskin had ordered the flowers? Was this some more upstage stuff? What right had he to waste the company's money in flowers to buy her off?

She took her seat with inward protest. This was going to be a most difficult luncheon, because he was making everything so absolutely perfect that it seemed to be the height of rudeness to hold herself aloof in this way, yet she knew she must do it. She must not let herself be hoodwinked.

His manner was perfect, pleasant, grave, not too friendly. He did not presume upon their introduction. Neither did he emphasize her connection with the home office. She felt almost embarrassed by his quiet dignity.

He gave the order without consulting her beyond asking, "You like chicken? And coffee, or iced-tea?" in a low tone as if he were a frequenter of the place and the waiter thoroughly understood his wishes. A delicious fruit concoction arrived almost immediately.

For the first few minutes he talked of commonplace things—the weather, her journey—and asked for details of Mr. Fawcett's accident. But when the main course arrived, and the waiter had left them alone he turned his keen eyes on her with a more human friendly look that she had seen in them since their eyes first met in the banquet hall.

"Will you tell me honestly just why you want to get rid of me?" he asked in a tone that was utterly disarming, and his eyes lost not a flicker of expression on her face.

The quick color came into her cheeks and she looked up with sudden confusion in her eyes, realizing that she was not here to have a good time socially, but to do her duty by her employer. How was it that this man had the power to make one forget that for the time? She must guard herself!

She pulled her thoughts together and answered stiffly:

"I've nothing against you personally, Mr. Duskin. But I was sent out here to serve the company's best interests, and I must do that of course, no matter how unpleasant personally it might prove to be."

She finished with more ease. It seemed to her she had done pretty well with that speech, although it rather choked her to try to take another mouthful, and she poised her fork over the delicate bit of chicken on her plate without making any move to carry it to her lips.

"And you think you can serve the best interests of the company by dismissing me?"

The quiet voice did not sound annoyed. His eyes were still almost amusedly on her face. It confused her to have to face that steady look.

"Why, certainly!" she answered sharply, dropping her own eyes to her plate. "You did not think I would have made that decision if I had not thought so, did you?"

"But why did you think so?" he asked with still that steady look, as if he were searching her.

"Because it is absolutely necessary that that building be finished on time. I feel that we must have someone on the job who will not be constantly balked by trifles. You read the letter that I brought from Mr. Fawcett?"

"I did," he said, "but it said nothing about dismissal. Did Mr. Fawcett tell you to dismiss me? If so why did he not put that in the letter?"

"The letter was written just before Mr. Fawcett's accident. He was about to take the train for Chicago, on his way here. I imagine the letter was to prepare you for some such thing. It was to have been mailed before he left, but in the confusion it did not get off, so he told me to bring it."

"And he told you to dismiss me?"

"Well, no, not in so many words. He gave me the power to act in any way I thought best to insure the completion of the job before the date set."

"I see!"

There seemed incredibly to be almost a gleam of satisfaction in the young man's eyes.

"And now, may I ask, before we go any further, whether you have ever had any special training in engineering and construction? Do you know, for instance, just how far along such a building as the one we are at work upon, should be at this stage of the game? Have you any practical reason for thinking it is not going to be ready at the time promised?"

She looked up defiantly.

"I have!" she said with a little tilt of her head.

"You have training?" he asked quietly.

Her eyes wavered and she tried to cover her confusion by words.

"No, I mean I have reason for thinking it is not going to be ready on time, and you know it means a large forfeit to the company if it is not. We are not risking it any longer."

"May I ask what your reason is?"

"We have had complaints, Mr. Duskin. The people most concerned are alarmed and anxious."

"I thought so!" was the unexpected response. "You have been talking to Schlessinger and Blintz. A pair of dirty crooks!"

"Isn't that rather a dangerous thing to say about the owners of the building you are at work upon?" asked Carol with a self-righteous tone she was far from feeling toward the two men who were haunting her steps.

Duskin laughed a big boy laugh of pure mirth:

"Dangerous?" he questioned amusedly. "If I had been worried about danger I would have quit long ago. But honestly, don't you know about those two men? Don't you know they are not the owners? Who told you they were? Did they?"

"Oh, no," said Carol quickly, "but I understood—"

"Yes, they've been making people understand all sorts of things, but the time is almost here when we can make a few things understood too, and show them up for what they are."

There was a dangerous light in his eyes and Carol could not help being impressed.

"What do you mean?" she asked, trying to put dignity into her voice and failing miserably. "Who are they?"

"Schlessinger is mayor of this blooming town, and Blintz is his henchman! That's who they are! They used to be a couple of gamblers who ran a so-called high-class place on the quiet. That is, Schlessinger owned it, and Blintz appeared to run it. They got themselves pretty well established, and got possession of a lot of other branch places, made a little money, and bought a lot of voters, and then Schlessinger got himself elected as mayor. This building we're putting up is for municipal purposes, and is to be paid for out of the city treasury, did you know that? And these crooks are getting as big a rake-off out of it as they can manage.

At least they are trying to do so, and they will go to all lengths to accomplish their purpose. And one of the best things they could do for that purpose would be to make the Fawcett Construction Company lose that forfeit! You can readily see that, can't you?"

"But surely," said Carol, wide-eyed, "they would be fools to do that! Wouldn't they be caught red-handed? Isn't the contract made public?"

"The contract and the results are *absolutely* in the hands of these two men!" declared Duskin. "They handle the business entirely, and the official board who are supposed to control them are hand and glove with them, and absolutely *bought up* by them! They will all share, of course, in the big rake-off! I have *evidence* of what I am saying."

Carol's eyes suddenly hardened. She remembered what Blintz had said about Duskin. She looked at the fine eyes, and seemingly strong face before her, and wondered that any man could be so completely masked. She remembered that even the devil was said to appear as an angel of light!

She drew a long breath and he saw her face harden.

"I am sorry," she said with an air of finality. "But I too have evidence of some things, and I cannot pass them by."

As soon as she had said that she was sorry. She had not meant to speak of that until she had told Fawcett himself about it, at least, not until the very last extremity.

A kind of surprise swept over Duskin's face.

"You—have—evidence—!" he repeated as if he could not quite fathom what she meant. He sat for an instant studying her, his expression changing so rapidly that she could not analyze its different meanings. The last one was almost stern. His eyes made her most uncomfortable. It was almost a scorn as when he had looked at her that night at the banquet.

"Meaning—?" he asked deliberately, and then answered his

own question, as if he had found the cue to it in her eyes. "You do *not trust me!*"

His eyes went down to the tablecloth where he flecked a crumb of bread into space, and then he lifted them again. His gaze was now inscrutable. She was too nervous to get its meaning.

"And may I ask what is your evidence against me?"

Carol drew herself up feeling absurdly inadequate to the situation. She seemed to have made a terrible muddle of this and scarcely knew where to take hold of the subject again.

"Mr. Duskin," she said desperately, "I would rather not talk any further about this matter. It would be better for both of us if we let this thing drop where it is. I am not ready to make public all that I know. I am not sure that it will ever be necessary."

"But you don't imagine, Miss Berkley," he said, with again that flash of almost amusement in the steel of his eyes, "that I am going to let the matter go at that? After putting in fifteen months of the best part of my life day and night, and fighting untold odds, that I am going to drop it all before I have fought it out to a finish? Just on a few words from an inexperienced girl who has got a few little lines on something she doesn't understand? When I promised Fawcett that if I lived I would see that this thing got done even before time! Don't you know that you and your foolish little dismissal is just one more of the countless hindrances that I've been up against since I began? If necessary I'll take the train back to New York tonight and see Fawcett in the hospital, and make him understand it all, but I'm not going to give up now. I've too much at stake!"

"Yes, I know you have!" said Carol, angry now, and very defiant. There was deep significance in her tone. He had called her a *little inexperienced girl!*

He looked at her again at that, and paused, taking it all in.

"So?" he said, and suddenly laughed, a pleasant mirthful

laugh, as if what she had said couldn't touch him at all. And as suddenly she felt that he was too nice to have done all that. She felt sorry for him. But she *mustn't* let this interest in him come to the front. It would be disastrous! She must finish the matter now once for all. She had gone so far, there was no turning back.

"Mr. Duskin," she said, lifting troubled eyes into which some of her sympathy had crept, "I'm very sorry, but I know all about it, and it will be much better for you to go. The evidence is most clear. And I may as well tell you that I have sent for another man to take your place. He will probably be here in the morning. His name is Delaplaine. Perhaps you have heard of him?"

Carol remembered afterward his expression as she said this like an indulgent parent taking blows in the face from a chubby baby hand. It both angered and puzzled her.

"I see," he said coolly. "Yes, I know him. We were in college together, and have kept up the acquaintance more or less since."

Then after a pause in which he deliberately took up his coffee cup and swallowed the last of its contents he said pleasantly, and quite as if nothing unpleasant had been going on:

"Well, shall we go?" He glanced at his watch. "My time is up. I'll have to get back on the job. That inspector promised to be in again at three o'clock. He didn't quite finish going over the work. I mustn't be late. He is just watching for a chance to make trouble for me. I can see you again after Delaplaine comes. May I call you a taxi?"

Dismissed, like a little girl who had been naughty, and sent back to her hotel in a taxi before she realized what was going on, or found words to stop it. And he walked off unscathed!

She could see him down the street in the sunshine lifting his hat to a trim little woman in black satin. He did not bear the marks of battle. Apparently she had not been able to reach him at all. From the start he had held the issue in his own hands and no matter what she did, he had turned it somehow to his advantage. Oh, he was a terrible man to be up against! With all her soul she rebelled against her situation. Why had she got meekly into that taxi, and let him order her off to the hotel? Why hadn't she stayed and made him own he was beaten? Why—?

But the taxi suddenly lurched to a stop in front of the hotel, and she almost went to her knees. Then when she attempted to pay the driver he said the gentleman had paid. That annoyed her too. She did not want to be beholden to him in any way. Now she would hurry in and if there was no message yet from Delaplaine she would call up New York on the telephone and try to get the doctor. Perhaps Mr. Fawcett would be able to talk with her. He likely had a telephone by his bed, and it surely would encourage him to know that she had made progress. She *had* made progress, she assured herself. Duskin was finally *fired!* He wasn't beaten but he was fired. He hadn't had a thing to say when he found who she had got to take his place. She was glad she had told him who it was. If she hadn't he might have been arguing yet.

Yet she had an unpleasant feeling that the interview was not concluded yet. She would have to explain to Delaplaine when he came, how hard Duskin had died, and that she had strong reasons for putting him off the job which she felt it was not her place to disclose until Mr. Fawcett was able to do it himself. As she stepped within the hotel corridor it came to her that if Delaplaine had not yet turned up she would try to get Frederick Fawcett and ask him to hunt him up in Chicago and see if he couldn't persuade him to take the midnight train. It really was time she had someone to advise with. Perhaps she had better confide in young Fawcett after all; he seemed pretty levelheaded. The more she thought about it the more she felt as if she had not finished with Duskin. The very set of his shoulders as he walked down the street had been defiant, like a rock that had never been moved, and would not and could not be moved whatever she did. She felt shaken almost to tears, though she despised a girl that cried. She was still ashamed of her breakdown the night she arrived.

Shutting her lips very firmly, and lifting her chin with determination, she swung around the corridor into the office to inquire if any mail was awaiting her, and came face to face with Schlesinger, in top hat and eyeglasses, looking more like a fox than ever!

Chapter 9

Philip Duskin passed a weary hand over his forehead and eyes before he put his hat back on his head. The black satin lady had passed on. He had not encouraged her to stop and talk with him though she would have liked to do so. She had met him at a dinner given by the mayor last week for the directors of a hospital of which her husband was one of the founders. He had been described to her as one of the rising young men of the times. He certainly looked it. She was glad her daughter Eleanor was coming home from an Alaska trip while he was here. They would give a dinner and a dance at once and invite him. He certainly was stunning.

But Philip Duskin felt anything but stunning as he passed on down the street. It was getting on his nerves, this continual procession of attacks from all sides. It was bad enough when it came from outsiders and crooks, but when it began to come from the home office things looked bleak. Of course this girl was simply trying to show off, letting the home office see what wonders she could work. She hadn't an idea how she was messing things, or would be messing them if he let her. He had not a moment's intention of letting her, of course, but it was going to be a lot of trouble to hinder her, and it would hinder himself in the bargain, and there was such a precious little margin of time left! It was too much that he must waste any on a silly girl who did not know what she was talking about. He had better try and get somebody on the telephone in New York and find out just how much authority she really did have. If she had been given carte blanche she might really make trouble, and he might even have to knock off and go to New York to see Fawcett at the hospital as he had threatened. This would be almost disastrous to the job. He really didn't dare be away a minute. Of course Bill and Charlie and the rest would stick by now that they were here, but what were they? Merely workmen with no authority. They would fight for him to the last breath in their bodies, but they couldn't do anything if the Schlessinger outfit took it into their heads to do something crooked.

Well, what was the use of worrying? This was only one more thing, the next hurdle to jump, the next ditch to cross; he couldn't afford to waste his strength thinking about it. If that girl kicked up a row, as she promised—and she likely would, he could see it in the set of her chin—he must have that wiring passed by the inspector so the elevator people and the trimmers could go ahead without him for a day. Every minute gained was two at the end, and he *must* put it out of his mind.

He swung himself onto a trolley car just as the door was about to close, and stood by the door ready to swing out again when his corner was reached. He couldn't even spare time to sit down and rest between blocks.

A young girl got on the car in a blue dress that made him think of Carol. How pretty she had looked with that blue dress just the color of her eyes, pretty and sweet and womanly, till she stuck up her chin and began to try to be his boss.

A grim smile dawned on his lips. "The little boss," he said to himself amusedly. She wasn't meant to be that! She had a face like a madonna! How many madonnas had the modern business world spoiled? And men too perhaps. How could a man work with a girl like that running around hindering? Of course she was smart and bright and all that. Doubtless a better businesswoman than many a man, but she was out of her place. He wasn't exactly an old-fashioned man who wanted women to be clinging vines, of course, nor to stick to nursing and housekeeping entirely. Women were bright and entirely capable of earning their own living, as capable as men when they had the same training. But the idea of sending this girl out on just her native grit and expecting her to run an important job like this was suicidal. Probably the office lost its head when Fawcett was hurt and they let her come.

You could see she was brighter even than most men, from the clever speech she made at the banquet, but, well, it must have gone to her head, this temporary little power, or else somebody had been feeding her a particular kind of propaganda to blind her eyes to the truth.

He frowned as he swung himself off the car at his corner and strode up the steps of the new building, looking at his watch and flashing a glance at the cars parked on the other side of the street. It was three o'clock, and that fellow wasn't here yet! Now if he shouldn't come at all he would have to waste more time hunting for him!

Two steps at a time he flung himself up to the second floor to question Charlie, not the least look about him of a man who had just been badly fired.

Half an hour late the inspector was, and a sullen look on his face. Duskin found him disposed to pettiness and faultfinding. But at every turn they balked him. Patiently they took up floor-boards to prove that all was as it should be according to the ordinance, cheerfully they pulled him up to the eleventh floor in the lift to make sure that something else was all right which he professed to have forgotten to look at when he was up there the night before. At last reluctantly, grouchily, he signed the papers, taking as long as possible. It was half past four before he was gone, and the carpenters had all gone too.

"Now, Dusky, let's get at them fixtures!" said Charlie with a gesture of relief. "Want I should slip down and bolt that there street door? Any danger of the lady boss arriving on the picture again?"

"No," said Duskin, a slow grin coming on his lips, "no danger any more. She's fired me. That's over, thank goodness."

"*Fired* you, has she? I'll *bet* she has, Dusky! You *look* fired, you do. Never saw you look more bullheaded than you do this minute, not even under shellfire. I'll say she's fired you. Fired you up, I guess! Only you didn't need it. If she asks me I'll tell her a thing or two."

"Keep your mouth shut," said Duskin amusedly. "You'll need your breath before we get through. All set?"

"All set."

"Had any sleep?"

"Five hours, Dusky. I'll bet it's more than you've had in as many days."

"On with the dance, then, Charlie. Top floor. I'd just as soon they didn't get onto it that it's so near done till we spring the whole show!"

"You've said it, Dusky. Hey, there, Pete, Ted, tell Bill to bring up the limousine from the garage."

The lift squeaked its thunderous way up from the cellar and Bill appeared cheerily whistling. They crowded in, shoulder to shoulder, the boss and his brother workmen. The weary lines of Duskin's face began to smooth out, and a look of peace and contentment to take their place.

"Now, Dusky," said Charlie springing out when they reached the top, "when you get this job up here laid out, you're to go over in that there corner and lay down! See? I come up here whilst you and the crab sided inspector was shooting off to one another, and I took the hay outta the fixtures' boxes and stirred up a bed for ya.

It ain't no fancy Waldorf Astoria, but it'll pass. And we agreed together, that you're to lay down an' get some rest till we're through up here, or we all quit on ya! Get me?"

"I get you!" said Duskin grinning with them. "All right, pile off, and we'll lay out the idea."

Carol was positively frightened when she came upon Schlessinger so unexpectedly. Being unstrung already with her interview with Duskin, she was hardly prepared to face another giant in her way. Schlessinger in his afternoon regalia looked every inch a mayor, the high gold bridge of his eyeglasses setting off the hawk nose to perfection. She had a wild hysterical idea as she faced his elaborate bow of crying out with Red Ridinghood, "What makes you have such a long nose, Grandmother?" but instead she tried to control her trembling lips and look like the stern representative from New York.

"Miss Berkley, I've been looking for you for several hours. I wanted to ask you to take lunch with me. Sorry I have somehow missed you. I wonder if we can go somewhere and have a little talk at this time?"

Carol summoned a smile:

"It will not be possible, Mr. Schlessinger. I have a very important matter to attend to at once. I am afraid I am late now. I can't tell how long it will take me."

"Now, that's too bad," he said vexedly, "because I have something quite important to say to you."

"I can't possibly wait," said Carol fearfully, backing away from him. "I'm sorry to be rude, but you know business matters won't wait. It's a matter of long-distance calls."

"I see," said Schlessinger, his hawk eyes upon her. "Well, I will walk with you to the elevator then and just say a word. I can't ask you to take dinner with me tonight because I have a municipal dinner to attend that I can't possibly get out of, and I'm afraid you wouldn't enjoy that, a dull stupid affair connected with a hospital, but I'll arrange to see you tomorrow, say at lunchtime. I'll come for you—at one o'clock, shall we say? And in the meantime, I just want to say this, I wouldn't want you to do a thing about upsetting young Duskin on the job because of anything I said. He's a well-meaning young man. It really would be useless anyway. Things are too far gone for that. The only thing you can do is to urge him to do his best. I have been troubled ever since at what I said to you in Chicago. At least what Blintz said. He is so impulsive."

Carol had put out a quick hand and signaled the elevator and it blessedly arrived now.

"Indeed, Mr. Schlessinger, you needn't be concerned at all about anything you said in Chicago. I am acting under orders from New York. I assure you that building is going to be done on time!"

Was she imagining it or did a spasm of anxiety flit over the fox face as she said that? She hastened on:

"And about tomorrow, I'm afraid I can't promise. I shall probably have another engagement for lunch. Thank you just the same."

"Well, I'll see you at one tomorrow, anyway, and we'll arrange it," insisted Schlessinger. "I hope you will find you can come then."

In a frenzy of haste she stepped far within the elevator and was thankful when the operator slammed the door shut and the car began to move. As she glanced out through the grillwork she could see the old fox standing baffled for an instant, and then he turned and walked straight over to two people who sat on a lounge across from the elevator. He nodded and seemed to motion toward the elevator. She caught a glimpse of a woman with white hair, a purple dress and hat, and a big jeweled lorgnette sitting beside a young man with a languid air who was reading a paper. Then she was taken swiftly up and promptly forgot all about it, thankful only that she had escaped as easily as she had. She would look out tomorrow that she did not encounter Schlesinger again and she would plan the day so full that she would have plenty of excuses at hand. But why had he said nice things about Duskin? It looked as though he really was afraid he would be dismissed. Were they then really in collusion?

Locked into her room she put in a call for Frederick Fawcett in Chicago, but after a half hour of waiting found he had gone to a house party out at some lake and would not be back till after the weekend. Succeeding at last in getting the house where he was a guest she was told that he was off on a fishing expedition in the woods, and would not return until sometime the next day. He was staying overnight at a cabin in the woods where there was no telephone.

Perplexed she sat on her bed and watched the sunshine come in longer slants across the rug and furniture as the day waned. What should she do next?

In despair she called the Delaplaine number again and was rewarded by a man's voice at last.

"Yes, this is Delaplaine. No, I didn't get your message yet, haven't seen anyone. I just got in. What's that? A *job?* A new operation? When does it begin? Tomorrow? What? Oh, it's almost done? Impossible! I never take over anyone else's job. Couldn't think of it. No! Besides, I'm off for a month in the mountains. Start tonight. Just finished a big operation myself. Wouldn't take another for a million dollars until I've had some rest."

Carol at the other end of the wire voiced her despair in such a plaintive tone that Delaplaine halted in his movement to hang up, and listened to her plea.

"Tough luck!" he said. "But I couldn't come in and pull up a thing at the last minute. Why didn't you find it out before it was too late? Who's your manager? What's that? Duskin? Not *Phil* Duskin? Why, ma'am, what do you want me for then? You couldn't have a finer manager in the country. What does he say about it? Does *he* want me? He isn't sick or anything is he? Because if Dusky was sick and needed me I'd give up a trip to Europe to help him. What's that? You've *dismissed* him? *Him?* And he said he was going to get it done! Why, my dear madam, don't you know that if Philip Duskin says a thing will be done at a certain time it will be *done,* even if there isn't a stone of the foundation laid the night before? Phil would lie down and *be* a foundation himself if it was necessary, but he'd get it done and maybe a minute and a half before the clock struck, too. *That's Duskin!* No, ma'am! If you people have been such darned fools as to dismiss Phil Duskin from your job you can go whistle for another man. I'll make it hot for you from one end of the country to another, I can tell you, too! Your company will never be able to get *any* of us to work for you again if you treat a prince of a man like Dusky that way. *I'm done.* Good-bye!"

Carol sat trembling on her bed for a full two minutes. What had she done? What could she do now? She mustn't let this go through. She had angered one of the best men in the country it seemed. What would Mr. Fawcett say when she got back? What would *all three* Fawcetts say? For Frederick Fawcett had made it quite plain that this Delaplaine was one of the best men to be had and that they were thinking of him for a big library they were to build soon. In fact they had opened negotiations with him. Suppose this ended that? It would mean that she would lose her job, if she wasn't able to apologize or in some way blot out the impression she had made. Oh! She must not let him go away angry that way. She must do something right away about it!

In a panic she seized the telephone again and asked in a queer little voice that was not in the least like her ordinary telephone voice at home, if they would *please* give her that long-distance number again, that the number had hung up before she finished talking.

After five long minutes of anxiety the same strong manly tones came over the wire, a bit cross:

"Well?"

"This is Fawcett Construction Company. You didn't understand me, quite, that is I didn't mean—that is—Mr. Duskin *isn't* exactly dismissed—*permanently.*"

"Oh!" the voice was somewhat sardonic. "Not *permanently.* How's that? Do you do it intermittently?"

Carol suppressed a desire to burst into hysterical giggles. What would they say in the New York office if they could hear their dependable, efficient, self-controlled secretary now? She had gone all to pieces.

"I beg your pardon," said Carol quite humbly, "I'm sorry I gave you such an impression. I suppose it must have been all wrong what I said, but I'm carrying a very heavy burden of responsibility, and I want to do the best thing for the company. You see Mr. Caleb Fawcett has met with an accident."

A sudden sympathetic voice over the phone:

"Is that so? I hadn't heard. That's hard now, isn't it? And you're sent out there to look after things? Did he ask you to phone me?"

"No, I heard Mr. Frederick Fawcett of Chicago speaking of you in high terms and I thought perhaps you might help out in this job. You see it means a great deal to the company to get done on time, and Mr. Fawcett's been worried nearly to death. He's had a lot of complaints from the people it's being built for—"

"Oh, it's that municipal job, isn't it? I remember. They asked me to take it but I was full up. But you say you've got Duskin. Didn't he have it at the start?"

"Yes, but there have been a lot of setbacks."

"There are always a lot of setbacks, my friend, on any operation! Don't let that worry you. Did Duskin say he needed help?"

"No-o-o!" admitted Carol sheepishly, feeling very small and ridiculous indeed, "but I thought—"

"Well, think again, my friend. You've got the best man I know on your job. When he wants my help he knows where to find me and he knows I'll come hopping. But he also knows I won't come before. And if he says it'll get done you might just as well pack your suitcase and go back to New York. Don't lose a drop of sleep on account of it. Duskin always puts a thing over! Good night! My train's leaving in a few minutes. Wish you luck!"

The receiver hung up and Carol said her mortified thanks to the world at large or the telephone operators.

Reluctantly at last she hung up, realizing there wasn't another thing she could do about Delaplaine, and that she had all she could handle right now in straightening out what she should do about Duskin. Somehow she had suddenly experienced a change of mind with regard to Duskin. Evidence or no evidence there had been no mistaking what Delaplaine thought of Duskin, and Fawcett had said that Delaplaine was a wonder. There was no use, she was in a terrible jam and that was all there was about it. She wished that she was at home. She wished she had never come. She wished she had her mother to comfort her. She wished she had followed Betty's advice and let the old construction company go to the dogs. She wished she had gone to the seashore in Maine with the rocks and the sand and the sad sea waves, and the excellent hotel in the background. And then she lost all respect for herself and flung her face down in the pillow and cried again.

She just simply couldn't do anything else. She who scarcely ever cried in her life had cried already twice on this miserable mission. It was high time she packed up and went home. She was doing worse than nothing. And now, how was she to get hold of Duskin? Somehow she must see him and placate him. It wouldn't do for the job to be left without a manager. *She* wouldn't know how to tell them to put in elevators, nor put on safety treads nor finish trim. Oh, if she only dared feel that the Lord would be her confidence as that verse had said. Her mother's Lord! But what could the Lord do in a case like this? She had never paid much attention to the Lord.

Humbled at last to the dregs of despair she began to realize that it was high time to get up and do *something.* Moreover she was very hungry.

She looked at her watch and found to her horror that it was half past seven. Six hours since she had eaten the excellent lunch at the University Club with Duskin. Well, Schlessinger was safely out of the way for the evening; she might venture down to the hotel restaurant and get her dinner. Then while she was eating she could make some plan about getting hold of Duskin. She wished she had an idea where he spent his evenings or where he boarded or something, but doubtless the hotel clerk could help her in that.

She put on the little black satin dress and the string of pearls. It seemed as if anything gayer would be out of keeping with so grave a situation. She looked very pretty when she was ready to go down, with her slim gray silk ankles and the little patent leather pumps with their bright buckles. She put on a close black satin hat with an arrow of rhinestones and took her black satin coat and handbag. As she turned to leave the room something made her turn back and hunt out her little flashlight that she had stowed in her suitcase for use on the sleeper. She had an idea back in her mind and the flashlight might be needed.

Then, hesitating, she paused beside the bureau where her Bible still lay open at the place, her eyes eagerly scanning the page again. She turned a leaf or two and read: "He that walketh with wise men shall be wise: but a companion of fools shall be destroyed." Well, there was nothing in that! She was not companioning with anyone just now, and not likely to. She closed the book and left the room with the reflection that it was superstitious to expect to find guidance for present-day problems in a book that was written thousands of years ago.

When the elevator reached the lower floor she glanced quickly about the room, and noticed two people sitting in the same seat where those two people had sat when she went up. Something familiar about them made her look again and see that one was a lady with white hair and a purple gown and lorgnette and the other a young man with a small mustache and a newspaper. They looked bored and tired and the lady was yawning, but she stifled her yawn and sat up suddenly as the elevator door opened.

As Carol passed by her she heard her say:

"Paisley, dear, do let us go out to dinner. I don't think it is of the least use to wait any longer for Annabel. She has probably gone with her cousin and I'm starved!"

Carol passed close by them and went to the desk. She wanted to ask the clerk to be looking up Duskin's address for her while she was at dinner. Then she passed on into the dining room.

She chose a table a little to one side where she felt she might be more to herself. But while she was studying the menu card she heard the purple lady's drawl close beside her.

"No, waiter. I want to get near an electric fan, I said. Here," and she turned toward Carol. "My dear, *would* you mind if we sat at your table? The room is so full, and I *do* feel as though I must have the air from one of the fans. You are all alone—or—were you expecting someone to join you?"

"Not at all," said Carol trying to sound gracious, but feeling dismay at the thought of having company just now when she wanted to think.

The two sat down with murmured thanks and Carol withdrew to her menu card. The young man adjusted his mother's long fringed white silk shawl, took charge of her handbag and her fan, picked up her handkerchief, and put her into her chair. He sat down himself. The two had not a little discourse over their order, and kept the waiter several minutes after Carol had given hers, deciding whether they would have artichokes or salad, and whether the iced-tea would be better than hot coffee. Carol sat impatient, and eager to be away, but she did not like to go to the length of getting up and going to another table, so she sat with half averted gaze watching the people about her.

But as soon as her unwelcome neighbors had arrived at an agreement concerning their dinner they sat back and smiled at her much as if she were their guest.

"It was perfectly darling of you to let us come here, my dear," said the lady, leaning over and touching Carol's shoulder lightly with her jeweled lorgnette. "I should simply have died of heat prostration over in the more crowded part of the room, and there wasn't another fan except where the tables were full. You're quite sure you won't mind?"

"It's perfectly all right," said Carol, trying to make it a matter of indifference, and smiling a trifle frigidly.

But the lady did not seem to feel the frigidity. Carol did not look at the young man to see whether he felt it or not.

"That's sweet of you," the lady said, "and I shall enjoy the evening all the more because you are young. I do so love young people. I'm quite provoked at my niece. She was to have met us for dinner tonight. But you will take her place. That makes it so nice. Are you a stranger in town, or an old resident? I don't think I've noticed you in the dining room before."

"I'm from New York," said Carol briefly.

"Oh, New *York,"* the woman fairly caressed the word. "You've wandered far. On a vacation I suppose? Are you alone?"

"I'm a businesswoman," explained Carol crisply, "and I'm here on business."

Would the woman never let her alone?

"Oh, really? How interesting," persisted the woman. "Oh, do tell me about it. All these things that women are doing in this wonderful generation are so perfectly fascinating! I said to Paisley the other day, 'Paisley, my son, you must really hunt up one of these interesting modern women for a wife. I'm dying to know one of them.' And here you are right by my side. Now, do tell me what you do?"

Carol avoided looking where the said Paisley was sitting. She did not know whether or not he relished being dragged into the conversation like this, but so far as she was concerned she let him see that he did not exist. This woman must be squelched in some way or she would have to get up and leave the room before her dinner came.

"I represent the Fawcett Construction Company of New York," she said quite coldly now, "and I'm here on business for Mr. Fawcett. I'm afraid you wouldn't be interested in the details."

Carol's voice was so aloof that it really put a period to the conversation and the orders arriving just then there was no further opportunity for the lady's volubility. But as soon as the dishes were arranged on the table, and the three had begun to eat, the lady leaned forward once more, her eyes sparkling with eagerness:

"My dear, I'm so excited I can't eat till I've settled it. Did you say the Fawcett Construction Company? Not the *Caleb* Fawcett Company! Don't *tell* me it *isn't!* It would be *too wonderful!*"

Carol had to admit that it was.

"But, my dear! Isn't this a coincidence! To think I should have met you this way! Why, my dear, I *went* to *boarding school* with Caleb Fawcett's *wife!* We are the *dearest* friends! Think of it! And that I should meet you this way and we should find it out! Oh, my dear! Do tell me how she is? You know her, don't you?"

"I have met her," said Carol remembering the efficient figure of Caleb's wife as she entered the office and took command of the situation. If this woman was a friend of Mrs. Caleb Fawcett's she would have to be at least polite to her. What a nuisance! It did seem strange that one couldn't go to a far city on business without meeting up with a lot of people that had to be avoided. Schlessinger and Blintz and this Paisley and his mother. Being friends of the Fawcetts made it a part of her job.

And now Paisley himself was brought into the conversation most adroitly.

"But really, my dear, we ought to know one another's name. I'm Mrs. Arthwait, and this is my son Paisley. We're *delighted* to meet you, aren't we, Paisley dear?"

"I'm Miss Berkley," said Carol reluctantly. What a lot of things she was getting into. What would her mother say?

Paisley proved to be rather a silent party. He assented to all that his mother said, ordered a bottle of wine, of which he offered to Carol and she declined. He smoked a good many cigarettes which he also offered to her and she declined. He told one or two harmless jokes and laughed a good deal. On the whole he did not figure heavily in the general accounting.

Carol hurried through her dinner as rapidly as possible, but so did her neighbors, and as she was preparing to leave the table Mrs. Arthwait leaned over eagerly and said:

"Now, Miss Berkley, you're going to give us the pleasure of your company the rest of the evening I'm sure. What shall we do, see a play or a picture, or just ride. It's almost too hot to stay indoors tonight, isn't it?"

"You'll have to excuse me," said Carol shoving back her chair. "I have to look up someone whom I must see tonight if possible."

"Oh, my dear Miss Berkley, then do let us help you. I'm sure we can help you. Let us take you to wherever you are going. Paisley has his car here, and it will be much pleasanter than riding in a taxi. Go get the car, Paisley, and bring it around to the front entrance. Oh, my dear! How pleased I am that we can do something for the friend of my dear old schoolmate. You must tell Mrs. Fawcett when you get back what a delight it was to hear about her again, and how glad I am we could do something to help you. She will remember me as Ida Lacey. Now, you won't forget to tell her will you? Shall we go out to the car now, or must you go upstairs again? Oh, I see you *have* a wrap, though you'll scarcely need it."

She chattered her way out to the car, and Carol much to her disgust found herself seated in a handsome car with Paisley Arthwait at the wheel and his mother beside her.

Well, perhaps, she reasoned, it was the easiest way to get rid of them. She would drive to Duskin's boarding place, the address of which the clerk at the desk had obtained for her, and there also would dismiss them. Then after they were gone she would do what she pleased.

Nevertheless, in spite of this reasoning, she felt a trifle uneasy driving off this way alone with utter strangers through a strange city. It was all nonsense, of course, but she kept thinking what her mother had said to her as she left her.

Then, strangely enough that Bible verse about companioning with fools kept coming to mind. Yes, she must get rid of them somehow right away.

She had put on her slim black coat, and pulled her hat down over her eyes, but still she could not get her mother's warning out of her mind.

So they drove away into the night.

Chapter 10

But the Arthwaits were not easily shaken. They insisted on waiting at Duskin's boardinghouse, to be sure that Duskin was there. In fact Paisley asserted himself and went to the door to inquire before he would let his guest alight from the car.

It was a plain little boardinghouse in a side street at which they stopped, and Carol had great doubts as to whether they had found the right place.

"Is this where Mr. Philip Duskin is staying?" she called from the car, to make sure.

The landlady was a quiet plain-faced woman, and the hallway behind her looked neat and clean and homelike, but not what she would have thought Philip Duskin would have chosen for even a temporary home.

"Yes, his name is Philip," the landlady said, "but he don't *stay* here, if that's what you mean. His trunk is here and he pays for his room, and he sometimes comes back to get a bath, but I haven't seen him for a week. He's been off to Chicago, and he's been working night and day. I'm sure I don't know how he stands it. I'm glad he ain't my son. I'd be worried to death about him. He don't look well, either. He's got dark circles under his eyes, and he hardly eats a bite, just drinks coffee and runs back when he does happen to be here for a meal."

"Do you know where I can find him now?" asked Carol feeling somehow as if she had been all wrong everywhere.

"Well, I reckon he's nowhere but on the job, unless he had to go out and cut down a tree to make more boards for the floor, or gather mud to make some bricks or something. He beats all for how he works. But I can't say where he is at present. If you leave your name I'll tell him when he comes in, but I can't say fer sure when that'll be. May not be fer a week."

Carol declined to leave a message, and she wished most heartily that she was rid of the Arthwaits. But when they begged to suggest a ride out into the suburbs, she declined and asked them to leave her at the building as she wanted to find out if anybody was there.

So they drove to the building, although the Arthwaits still would not leave her, and compromised by insisting on waiting for her.

There was a dim light in the lower floor, and Carol as she picked her way up the steps feared that the door might be locked, and that no one would hear her knock. But it chanced that the door was ajar, for the boy from the restaurant in the next block had forgotten to slam it behind him when he came down after delivering the evening ration of coffee and sandwiches.

Carol stole in and looked about her. Even in the one day since she had been there she recognized changes. A handsome bronze grillwork had been set up around the first floor elevator shaft, and although the doors were not in yet it began to take on the semblance of what it was to be. Also there were finished outlets in the walls where the day before there had been only protruding wires. Well, her coming had at least hurried up some things. What a pity someone had not come on from the office sooner.

She had closed the door behind her, for she was almost afraid Mrs. Arthwait might insist on coming up with her, or appear on the scene unannounced, or worse still, send Paisley.

She took a step or two forward into the hall expecting to hear the janitor come forward, and then she would ask him to go after Mr. Duskin. When no one appeared she finally called out several times, but there was no response, and the echoes of her voice died away into seemingly realm upon realm above. It gave her a weird feeling to be alone in this great empty unfinished building. In a finished building one knew what to count upon, but here there seemed to be pitfalls on every side. Nevertheless she did not intend to give up. She must see Duskin before morning. There was no knowing what might happen to the job, now that Delaplaine had declined to come, if she let Duskin go. For Duskin was at least a figurehead. Men would not work without someone who stood for boss. She must keep him until she found out what else to do.

Finally, though she shuddered inwardly, she went forward to the elevator shaft and peered up. Far, far above, like a moon above a deep, deep well she saw a dim square of light, and heard echoes of voices, but when she tried to call again her voice came back like a rubber ball that had hit against the wall.

Then she resolutely turned back and went to the stairs. Dared she go up that way? How many flights would it be? Schlessinger and Blintz had climbed up once. If they could surely she could. Suppose she should meet someone in the dark on the stairs? Suppose she should meet Schlessinger and Blintz! Even the eager Arthwaits could not help her for they would never hear her cry for help. Her voice would be drowned in that great marble lined tunnel. Nevertheless she meant to go.

She crept on up higher, and the dim light from below failed entirely. Then she snapped on her flashlight and held it above her head, climbing, climbing, millions of steps, turning around another hallway, and more steps again. She had lost count of the stories. It seemed like the very tower of Babel, and her limbs were trembling and almost numb. Her heart seemed to be pumping her breath from away down in the foundations of the building somewhere, and once or twice she sat down on a step to rest.

The last time she sat down she heard voices, and turning off her flash she perceived that there was a dim radiance from the story above. Her climb was almost over. But she must sit still a moment and get her breath. She did not wish to appear before Duskin entirely winded. He would think her a fool. Perhaps she was but she did not want to appear like one.

Then as she rested halfway up the next and last flight she heard voices again, more distinctly now, just above the turn of the stair it seemed. They were talking in subdued tones, but the words came distinctly down the marble well in which she sat.

"Naw, don't wake him, Charlie. I don't give a hang if you did promise. We can get this part of the work done between us, easy. I tell ya, Charlie, he's all in. He ain't had any sleep fer five nights, and if that lady boss comes around bothering him like a hornet t'morra, no telling where he'll be."

"Yes, but he's had a sleep, Ted, and he said two hours was all he'd allow. You know as well as I do Dusky cares more about getting this here shack done on the tap than he does if he ever gets any more sleep. You know what he is. And I tell you he'll never trust me again if I don't come on time. Besides, Ted, he's gotta get this done before t'morra. Nobody else could fix this layout the way it oughtta be, and there's no telling what that flip little dame will do when she gets here. I ain't expecting her to be anything but a consarned nuisance, of course. When they get skirts on a job like this you gotta expect trouble. Course Dusky don't mind that part. He's usedta gnats and hornets and things. But I tell ya what I'm pretty well convinced of myself. I donno whether the boss has thought of it or not, but I'll bet my bottom dollar that little dame is in with the ring and going to get her rake off out of this here grab game outta that forfeit money. She looked ta me like a cute one. And those two dirty crooks that's running this here gag business ain't going to waste any time getting her bought over, I'll tell the world."

"She didn't look to me exactly that kind," demurred Ted, "I think she was *just dumb.*"

"Aw, don't be an *infant,* Teddy. Where's she get all them glad rags? It takes money to buy cloes like that, son, and she'll be only too glad to grab all she can get. I tell you, son, Dusky is the only man I know outside this here outfit of his, that won't turn a hair when they offer him a kingdom. You'd oughtta seen his face, the day old Schless made an offer of his third of the forfeit! Oh, boy! I was workin' up in the ceiling above his head, and the hole where the chandelier was goin' was plenty big to give me a pretty good bird's eye view of the scene. Good night! I thought that rotten old crook was goin' to fall all the way downstairs, the way he lit out when Dusky took him by the collar and shook him over the stairs. Oh, boy! If that little dame that thinks she can boss him had a' been present at that scene she wouldn't 'a come around here in her jazzy cloes and her high-heeled shoes with shiny buckles holding her chin so high and mighty! The dirty little crook! I don't care if she is a girl! She's a dirty little crook or she would know enough to know there ain't anyone this side glory as good as our boss. She ain't fit to let him wipe his good honest shoes on her. She's a dirty little crook or my name ain't Charlie McMurray."

Cautiously, stealthily, when she had gathered breath, and could still the trembling of her limbs, Carol crept back, down the long long flights, painfully, breathlessly, hearkening fearfully now and again at a sound from above.

She did not dare turn on her light, but crept along the walls by feeling, and down upon her hands and knees found the next set of steps. Once her flashlight slipped from her shaking fingers, and rolled down two steps before she could get it again, and she stood with bated breath and listened to see if anyone had heard.

Till at last she gained the hall below, and the dim light, and fled to the front door and out, closing it noiselessly behind her.

Oh it was good to breathe the fresh night air again, and to feel a breeze upon her hot forehead and burning cheeks. Would she ever forget the things those men had said?

She steadied herself an instant before going down the steps to the car. She was grateful to these strangers for waiting for her, now, for she felt she could not have walked and had not wits enough left to call a taxi. She was glad it was dark, and they could not see how agitated she was. She got into the car, and tried to speak steadily, though her voice sounded a little strained.

"Now, if you would be kind enough to take me back to the hotel," she said, "I'm suddenly very tired. I've had a hard day, and I think there's another one ahead of me tomorrow, and I need some rest."

They were most assiduous and eager. She thought how ungrateful she must be not to appreciate their kindness, but she simply longed to get away from them, and when at saying good night they begged that they might be allowed to take her to dinner the next night and show her a good time somewhere, she, remembering Schlessinger and eager for some excuse to get away from him, accepted.

And so she was allowed at last to go to her room, and shut herself in with the memory of her day—and evening!

When she snapped on her light and sat down to examine the mail she had brought up from the desk she found two telegrams among them.

One from Caleb Fawcett:

"Cannot understand why I do not hear from you. Wire immediately giving fullest particulars."

The other from the doctor:

"Very important that you keep Fawcett easy in mind. The right message will pull him through. Make it peppy and daily. Twice a day if possible."

She sat staring at them after she had read them, and felt as if this was the last straw in a day that had been all failure from beginning to end. She had utterly forgotten that some message should have gone to Fawcett that morning, or at least sometime during the day. Now she had a vision of the placid Mrs. Fawcett and an impeccably trained nurse endeavoring to quiet the irascible Caleb while he raved on demanding telegrams from the West. Her worn-out nerves broke into a laugh, which was almost on the verge of tears.

Of course, she must send him a telegram before she slept, but what could she say? If she gave details as he asked it certainly would be "peppy" enough to suit the most exacting, but not, she imagined, the kind of "medicine" the doctor would care to have administered. She had sent a telegram from Chicago the morning after the banquet, describing in glowing words the good fellowship toward the company, and telling of the speech she had tried to make, and how well it was received. It had been carefully studied to relieve her employer's mind about the situation in Chicago, and let him see that his absence had not been entirely fatal so far as his interests were concerned. She had also sent a telegram the afternoon she arrived in this town, giving her location and saying that she intended to see Duskin at once and get things to moving rapidly, as she had learned several things in Chicago which she felt would materially help to solve difficulties.

But now she saw that Fawcett was no more in a frame of mind to accept such sugar-coated generalities than he was when he was actively in the office, swearing at everybody that crossed his purpose. She must be definite if she would help him get well, and yet she must tell him nothing to worry him. And her mother had brought her up to tell the truth. How were all three of those things possible? And yet it must be done.

Without waiting to remove her hat and coat she took a pencil and pad from her suitcase and began to scribble telegrams, tearing them up and consigning them to the wastebasket as fast as she wrote them. At last in despair she lay back on her bed and stared up at the ceiling. She simply had got to get things thrashed out in her mind before she went a step farther. The telegram would not be delivered in a hospital at that hour of the night anyway.

At two o'clock she finished the draft of her telegram and stirred up a sleepy night operator to get it off. It read:

> Been busy all day getting acquainted with operation. Work progressing better than we thought. Duskin on job day and night, feels certain all will be done on time. Electric wiring completed and passed inspection. Elevators being put in today which will greatly expedite further work. (Carol wasn't just sure whether that was so or not, but it sounded well). Expect to spend tomorrow on the job, and will have full details by next week. No cause to worry. All seems to be going well.
>
> (Signed) C. Berkley.

After she had sent her telegram she read her mother's letter enclosing one from Betty. They were both full of plaints and warnings, and begged her to get done her work as soon as possible, delegate it to someone else if she could, and come on back home. There was still time to go to Maine. Jean had telegraphed that they wanted her even if it was only for a few days.

She sighed as she folded the letters and stuffed them under her pillow for company. How horrified her mother would have been if she could have known how she spent part of her evening. What would her mother have said if she could have heard the awful words those men had said, calling her a "dirty little crook!" Her cheeks burned anew with the memory of their contempt. No wonder her mother felt that she was not fit to go out alone in a world of men. Mothers knew what evil was in the world, as no one could know without experiencing it perhaps. Oh, but the experience was bitterly gained! She felt that she was permanently saddened by the view she had heard of herself in the words of those unspeakable men. To think that any man, no matter how bad he was, could think of her in that way! And yet, those men did not seem like bad men. They were evidently honest men themselves, or seemed to think they were.

Thoughtfully she undressed and crept into her bed, trying to plan out tomorrow. Somehow she must get hold of Duskin at once in the morning and see that he went on with his work. Compel him to whether he would or no.

No, that wouldn't do. You couldn't compel a man like Duskin. It might be that he would refuse after what she had said to him.

Toward morning she dreamed that she was having a long hard fistfight with Duskin on the stairs of the new building, that she struck him with all her might, but it only sounded as if she were patting a cushion, and that he struck her softly as if he did not want to hurt her, but now and again the lights would go out in the building and they would roll down a few flights of stairs, and then get up and go at it again. At last they reached the first floor and he caught her and carried her into the room they used for an office, and tied her hands and feet with electric wire that lay in great coils on the floor, and threw her into a corner with his coat folded under her head for a pillow. He told her she must stay there until the last day of September when the building would be finished and she might go home. She was terribly worried about the telegrams that wouldn't get sent to Fawcett, and when she told Duskin he only laughed and fed her with mush and milk, using a piece of building paper for a spoon, and the milk ran down her chin.

She woke up laughing, and jerked herself up into a sitting posture.

"Carol Berkley, if you're going to get hysterics," she said aloud, "you'd better go home today and own yourself beaten! You can't put anything over with your nerves all frazzled out like this. You've got to buck up."

A glance at her watch showed it was eight o'clock, and she had meant to be on the job by this time. She sprang up quickly and dashing into her bathroom took a cold shower. That brought a reaction, and she felt better. She telephoned down for coffee and rolls to be sent up, and to save time ate while she was dressing, a bite between everything she did.

It was a warm morning, and breathless, demanding thin garments. She put on her little rose-colored silk crepe sports dress, and a broad hat of transparent white, rimmed and tied about with rosy velvet ribbon. It wasn't at all the sort of dress for a businesswoman to wear on a job. But she hadn't a suitable thing with her. If things went on much longer she must go out and buy a plain sensible dark blue or black frock she supposed, but since she had nothing more suitable, why not wear the prettiest? Since she could not wear these confections of clothes on the seashore as she had planned, why not enjoy them by herself while she fought her desperate battle in this strange city?

Before she left her room she dashed off a cold little note to Schlessinger to leave at the desk as she went out, saying that business matters would prevent her accepting his kind invitation for lunch.

Then she wrote a hurried note to Duskin to be sent up to whatever part of the building he was in. Not again did she propose unnecessarily to expose herself to the gossip of those unmannerly men. Her cheeks burned as she thought of them.

My dear Mr. Duskin:

I have been thinking over what you said yesterday and have come to the conclusion that it is unfair to you to make a change at this time. I shall, therefore, be glad to have you continue in your position of manager for the present at least, and will do my best to help you in every way. I would like to speak with you at once for a few moments and will wait downstairs until you can leave what you are doing.

Sincerely,
CAROL BERKLEY

As she was going out the door pondering what she had written, it seemed to her that she had been rather too informal in the letter, but there was no time to go back. She must hurry to the building. There was no telling what Duskin might have taken it into his head to do if he was still angry with her.

She went downstairs hurriedly, by the side entrance again, and took a taxi to the building. She was running no more risks of meeting Schlessinger and the Arthwaits. She had serious business ahead.

Arrived at her destination she found the place simply swarming with workmen. For some minutes she could not even get near the steps. Six men were carrying in great bronze grills, obviously a part of the elevator system. When the doorway was finally cleared and she stepped inside the hall she found it fully occupied with workmen placing and arranging the parts of the elevators. There was no room to pass them to the back of the hall where she had found the man mixing paint on her former visit. She had to step within the doorway of the front room on the left of the entrance to get out of the way of a great packing case that was being rolled into the hallway.

There was nobody in this room. It seemed to be used as a sort of office, although there were piles of trim and molding across one end, and boxes of screws and knobs and hinges lying around in little heaps at intervals on the floor.

There was an old cheap desk of pine, its drawers pulled out and bulging with papers, its top also piled high with letters, circulars, and papers. A man's dark blue serge coat was folded neatly on the top and a much thumbed panama hat atop of it. There were two cheap oak chairs and a locked safe in one corner. That was all.

She stepped to the back of the room to see if there was egress to the hall from the other door, but the way was entirely blocked. It was some time before there was opportunity to interrupt the noisy workers in the hall to inquire for the janitor, but at last the big trucks from before the door thundered on their way, and the hall was cleared of all but the regular workmen, and she ventured once more on a search for the man they had called Bill.

She found him in a little dark room in the subcellar filing a saw for one of the carpenters. He agreed to take the note up when he got the saw done, as the carpenter was in a hurry for it. Ten minutes Carol stood in that dingy basement, watching her letter as it lay among the filings, and waiting for Bill, while the file gave forth heart-rending sounds that rasped every nerve in her body. She would not leave until she was sure Bill had taken her letter, and meantime she looked around upon the solid masonry, the network of pipes and tubes and wires. What a work it had been to bring that great mass of materials to even this stage of perfection! She had never realized before what lay beneath the mighty structures of the world.

But at last the saw was filed, and she saw Bill take her dainty envelope between a grimy thumb and finger, blow off the steel filings, and carry it and the saw over to the lift.

"You better go back up the ladder," he indicated a rude stair down which she had crept. "Tain't no place for a lady up by them shaf's now. You better go home, lady! This ain't no place fer a woman. Nor today, 'specially. Too much goin' on. Get yer cloes all messed up!"

"Thank you," said Carol sweetly, "I have to see Mr. Duskin at once. I will wait in the office for him to come down."

"Suit yerse'f, lady, you may have a long wait."

So Carol climbed her way gingerly up to the office again, and sat down in one of the two oak chairs, to wait for Duskin, more aware than ever that her rose-pink sports costume was out of place on a job like this.

Chapter 11

It was ten o'clock when Carol glanced at her wristwatch and settled down to wait for Duskin. At twelve when the workmen all knocked off and sat around on the floor in the hall with their backs against the wall and brought out huge sandwiches and bottles of cold coffee and hunks of cheese, she was still there waiting.

Bill had brought up the note holding it in the tips of his grimy thumb and finger just as he had started with it, much as if it were something that might explode.

"Where's the boss?" he asked when he arrived at the top with his lift. "Lady boss sent me this up. She's waitin' down in the sub fer a nanswer! You wantta be quick about it, too."

Duskin turned grinning and looked at the letter.

"Stuff it in my pocket, Bill, I've got my hands full now. I'll read it when there's time."

"She's gonna wait till you come."

"All right. Get her a chair, Bill."

Bill hung around a few minutes, but the boss hadn't read the letter. He was moving a great pile of trim and lumber from a room where the painters were to come. He did not read the letter until the lumber was all moved.

Charlie was watching him out of the tail of his eye, his canny Scotch eye.

A twinkle dawned over Duskin's face, and fled like the dart of a hummingbird, something golden to see in its flight. Charlie began to hum a bonny tune.

The twinkle had left Duskin's face and taken some of the worn lines with it.

Duskin took a pencil out of his pocket and looked about for stationery. There was nothing in sight but Ted's empty doughnut bag. Duskin tore a bit off where there was the least grease and wrote:

> Have been working on the job right along, and expect to till it's done, but I haven't time to stop and talk now. Sorry. Don't worry.
>
> DUSKIN.

"Hey, Bill!"

"Right ho!" said Bill appearing instantly at the door. As if Duskin hadn't known what he was there for all the time!

"Deliver the answer, please."

Duskin went back to work and Bill drifted slowly down on his lift, and in due time delivered the old bit of brown paper with its message.

At first Carol was very angry. She had waited so long already that it seemed her patience had ceased to be a virtue, and she was on the qui vive to get to work. There would be things she should do of course. For one thing this room needed putting in order. There were unopened letters on that desk, and letters that wore the air of having been abandoned before they had been answered. That was something just in her line, and she ached to get at it if for nothing else than to rebuke this paragon of a manager who seemed to think he knew it all and she was an upstart to come in here and give him orders. But there was something in Duskin's glance as she remembered it that kept her from touching his papers without his permission. His presence seemed to linger in his domain and patrol the place for him about as well as if he had been there.

Carol read the brown paper message over several times, taking in everything there was about it. The almost insolence of keeping her waiting so long, and then the out and out insolence of telling her he had been on the job right along and meant to stay there till it was done. It was as much as to say that she had nothing to do with the matter anymore than a fly on the wall. She really hadn't made much headway after all, and perhaps she had been wrong in lowering her dignity and retracting her dismissal of yesterday. Oh, it was most humiliating. She had a feeling that he meant it to be.

Well, perhaps she had humiliated him—several times—without realizing it. Probably Mr. Fawcett's letter cut deep, too.

And then what he overheard her say in Chicago. It was all most unfortunate. It spoiled the thing from the beginning. And after all, wasn't she more offended because she felt she was a woman and therefore should be well treated whatever she did? Well that wasn't right after all. But he really was being insolent now toward the company. She represented the company, no matter how poorly, and he had no right to ignore her this way.

She went through various stages of indignation, righteous and otherwise, while she sat for another hour waiting. Incidentally she had opportunity to note that a great many men were very hard at work on a great many different parts of that building, and that they were not loafing on the job. Moreover things were getting done before her very eyes. Two more trucks arrived bearing great sheets of what looked like marble, which were carried in noisily and steadily by strong men, breathing heavily, great lungs puffing with hot breath, great hearts pumping fast under the heavy burden! She had never realized before how many burden bearers it took to complete just one little operation in the world, and there were so many millions of other operations. Why, the universe was like a great anthill of workers, each one doing his little part, giving his time and strength and brain and muscle to make the world a success. And when one worker fell down on his job how it tied up all the rest!

Then suddenly it came over her how like a panorama things were moving on in this building. The elevator workers had arrived along with the material they were to put up, and now, on the very heels of the great sheets of marble came a troop of men in white overalls and little white caps, who began to mix cement in a great rough box they brought, and manipulate those slabs of marble till they became a shining lining to the wall about the stairway. Everything was moving like clockwork, and yet the boss had not once appeared on the scene. He must after all have been a pretty good manager, for all these things could not just have happened.

Was it just by chance that her eye fell on that moment upon an open page of a letter lying on top of the pile of papers on the table? It was from a well known millwork firm in Chicago, and it stated:

> We are very sorry to have to tell you that we shall be delayed in sending the arched window sash which you ordered from us two months ago for the lower floor of your present operation. We are the only firm in this part of the country making that particular style of window, and it has been in great demand of late. We regret to say that we are behind in our work because of a mistake in an order that was sent in by telephone, and therefore we shall not be able to send yours as soon as we promised them. It will be at least three weeks before we can touch them. Regretting, etc.

Carol lifted her eyes instinctively to the wall, and there were the windows! She glanced back to the letter which she found was dated only a week ago, and then she stared up at the windows again, with their mullioned arches.

Was that one of the million little details that he had had to set right? And if it was how had he done it? If as the letter stated they were the only makers of such windows in that part of the country how had he procured them so soon? Here they were, already fitted into their frames and started on their life work and only one short week from the time the letter was written! Well, it must be magic. Either he had known some way to compel the firm to furnish them or had found some other place to get them. Her thoughts began to work on a number of things, beginning back with those rivets that had not arrived, and the paint that had been stolen nine months or more ago. Could it be possible that someone was systematically at work trying to keep that building from being finished on time?

Just then Bill came in stealthily on his rubber soles and took up the telephone, calling a number.

"Hey, you, Saxe! Is that Saxe! Well the boss says if you can't have them fixtures here fer the side walls in the Duskin building by three o'clock you needn't send 'em atall. He says he ain't fooling with you anymore. This is the third time you've disappointed him. He's going out elsewhere and get 'em, if they don't get here on the dot. The men are ready fer 'em now, and we ain't paying men to wait."

Bill slung the receiver in with a swank and was just shambling out again when Carol rose with an imploring gesture:

"Oh!" she said earnestly. "Will you please let Mr. Duskin know that I'm still here waiting. I know he's busy and mustn't be disturbed, but I thought perhaps he had forgotten about me, and it's really quite important. I have to send a telegram to the home office and I must see him first. Doesn't he ever go out for lunch? Is there some other exit and have I missed him?"

Bill looked at her as if he had just noticed her.

"Oh, you here yet?" he asked. "Wal, I dunno about the boss. He's pretty busy. Naw, he ain't forgot. He don't never seem to forget. But I guess he ain't had time yet. No, he don't go out for lunch regular. He only eats when it's handy. Never saw anyone like him. Reckon he thought you had got tired and quit however."

"I said I would wait, and I intend to keep my word," said Carol with dignity. She was tired and hot and discouraged, and she couldn't see her way out of this turmoil into which she had been sent.

Perhaps the thorny Bill saw the downdroop of her tired young lips and had compassion, for as he turned away he said:

"Wal, ef I see him when I'm called up again I'll try an' remember an' mention it to him that I see ye." Then Bill ambled away.

When the noon hour came the great building grew appallingly silent as saw and hammer and the various other instruments of labor were laid aside, and the men sat down to lunches or trooped off to restaurants.

Duskin, hard at work in the upper regions, paused, took out the note from his pocket and read it again thoughtfully. Then put it in his pocket and smiled to himself.

Charlie watched him furtively. They were alone in the room just now, and Charlie was privileged.

"'Smatter, Dusky? Got yer walkin' papers again?"

Duskin grinned appreciatively:

"Why, no, Charlie, I'm hired again! What do you think of that!"

"Hired again? By the lady boss? Now ain't she tricky? Whaddaya know about that, Dusky? She's learnin' her onions, ain't she? What ya going to do about it, Dusky? Accept?"

"Accept, Charlie, how can I? Why I never accepted the firing, so I couldn't be hired over again, you know."

"Right you are, Dusky. But what's going to happen next?"

"Why, you're going down to lunch, Charlie, and bring me up a doughnut, but on your way just cast an eye into the office and see how it goes with the lady. She's probably got tired and gone home."

Charlie took off his overalls, put on his coat and disappeared downstairs. Half an hour later he was back. Bill was still enjoying his noonday meal reeking with bacon and onions which he cooked in back of the furnace on a little gas hot plate, and Bill had not been called upstairs with the lift since his interview with the lady. Besides he figured that the boss did not want ladies around and the longer she had to wait this time the less likely she was to return another day, so he cooked his leisurely lunch and enjoyed it on an old cot behind the furnace.

"Well," said Charlie, arrived at the top where the boss still worked tirelessly screwing on little outlet plates and other fittings, "Rosebud's still there!"

"What?" said Duskin a little sharply, eyeing Charlie with a frown.

"I mean the lady is waiting patiently, and the whole place looks like a garden since she's come. She's dressed like a bonny flower, Dusky, and no mistake. It's a pity of her to have to waste that outfit on the empty office. But I think you've over calculated, Dusky! I think she'll be there waitin' when you go down, tomorrow morning. Do you want an extra custard pie for her, Dusky, tonight when I go out to eat?"

"Well, you're all right, Charlie, but you must remember she is our boss. She was sent here for that purpose."

"Oh, is she, Dusky? I didn't realize that. Then you're *our* boss and she's the *lady* boss. I'll try to remember that. Well, she ain't dressed fer the part, that's all I've got to say. But I think she means to stick it out if it's all next week."

"All right, Charlie, I'm going down now. I thought she'd get tired waiting, and you know I haven't any time to waste, but she really ought to have some lunch so I'll go down and see if I can make her go and get it."

"Good idea, Dusky, but while you're gone, take a bite yourself. You may not be hungry but you look it!"

Duskin laughingly laid down his screw driver and went downstairs. He walked and did not call Bill from his dinner. He could smell the onions and he knew what Bill was doing. So Bill missed a chance to deliver his message, which was a great deprivation to Bill.

Duskin came into the office so quietly that Carol did not see him until he stood before her. He noticed with compunction that she looked tired, and that there were tiny circles under her eyes as though she had not slept well.

"I am truly sorry," he said humbly, "I thought I made it plain that it was impossible for me to come down this morning. I was doing most important work, and I felt it was better to get it done than to waste precious time in getting our relative status in the matter settled satisfactorily. But I did not mean to be rude."

She looked up with a start as he spoke, and when she lifted her eyes he saw that they looked almost sad as if she were discouraged.

"It is quite all right," she said quietly, with none of the arrogance of the day before, "I rather expected to have to wait—some time!"

"You are a pretty good sport!" he said looking down at her with genuine admiration and something in his tone that seemed to hand back her self-respect.

A hint of a smile of acknowledgment hovered on her lips.

"Thank you," she said gravely, "but let us not waste time in compliments. I won't keep you any longer than is necessary, but I must know a little more about things than I do, and I must have some plan of action. Can you spare five minutes?"

He looked at her gravely.

"It would take more than five minutes to put you in possession of much knowledge or help you to lay out a plan of action," he said gently. "I am sorry, but I ought not to spend a minute more than I can help away from upstairs. You want a few general statements to give to Mr. Fawcett, I presume. If I sent you a few lines by this evening indicating what has been finished, and what is still ahead of us with the time it will probably take, will that be sufficient? It is late and you really ought to have some lunch, you know. I wish I might have the pleasure of taking you out, but I simply ought not."

"I'm afraid that wouldn't do, Mr. Duskin," said Carol earnestly. "There are a lot of things I must tell you, and talk over. Aren't you going to eat any lunch yourself? Don't bother about me. I often go without. Couldn't I sit with you while you eat, even if it is only a few minutes?"

"I'm afraid not, Miss Berkley. I can't spare time to go uptown and there are nothing but hot dog stands down this way."

"I've eaten hot dogs," said Carol smiling bravely. "Come on. I'm sorry to force myself upon you in your lunch hour but there seems to be no other way."

"Well, you *are* a good sport!" he reiterated, a new admiration in his eyes. "All right, wait just a minute till I get these togs off!"

He picked up his coat and walked away to a room at the back of the hall, and she could not help noticing how the grace of the gentleman was as apparent in overalls as in evening clothes.

He was back in a minute looking quite dressed up in a very seedy dark blue serge of a cheap variety.

"I'm hardly fit to go out with you," he said with an apologetic glance down at himself, and a look of deference toward her pretty frock and hat.

"Don't worry about me," she said rising, "I haven't anything but fancy rigs along with me, or I wouldn't come down here looking like this. My trunk was packed to go on a vacation at a summer hotel, when I was sidetracked here, and I hadn't time enough even to snatch a couple of old dresses and bring them along. I must send back for something if I have to stay long."

"Please don't!" he said quickly, "unless perhaps these things will get spoiled. It's a great refreshment to see something pretty and bright."

She flashed a look of surprise at him, but almost immediately they turned into the luncheonette and he said no more till they were seated and had given their order for hot cakes and hot sausages, the only viands the place afforded.

"Now," said he glancing at his watch, "what do you want of me? I can give you fifteen minutes, but no more."

Carol was ready for him. She had thought it all out during her long wait.

"I want three things," she said resting her chin on her hand and her elbow on the dirty counter, and talking eagerly. "First, I want someone detailed to take me from the top to the basement of the building and show me everything. It must be someone who knows, and can answer *all* my questions and tell me things that I don't know enough to ask. I would like that to be done this afternoon if possible. It is a part of my job, that I was sent here to do, and I must inform myself about every detail."

He bowed gravely.

"I had better do that myself," he said after an instant's thought. "No one else knows everything about it. How would this evening do? You can't be going about among all those men. Some of them are a pretty tough bunch. My evening gang are all right, but I can't answer for some of the others."

Carol flushed as she remembered some things she had heard his evening gang say, but she did not flinch.

"I have to work among men all the time at home," she said. "You have to forget such things when you are in business. But the evening will do, if that will suit you better. I did promise to go to dinner with some people, but I can call that off."

"On no account," said Duskin quickly. "Suppose we say five o'clock? Will that be too late for you?"

"No, that is all right, but I'm not so keen about the dinner. The people are strangers to me, an old schoolmate of Mrs. Fawcett's. I think she is just trying to be kind to me."

"I am glad you have friends here; it will not be so lonely for you. Don't give up your engagement. We can manage it, although you have outlined a pretty large proposition and we'll need some time. You couldn't wait till tomorrow afternoon could you? Tomorrow is Saturday, and the men knock off at twelve, all but my gang who are with me day and night whenever I choose to work. I shan't be quite so rushed then, either. We are trying to get ready for the painters who are promised Monday morning, and I think we'll be all in good shape by tomorrow morning. I always try to get a free mind for Sunday so I can rest up a bit."

She looked up at him thoughtfully.

"Yes, I think tomorrow afternoon will be very good. I will telegraph Mr. Fawcett that he shall have full details after tomorrow. I think that will satisfy him. I had a telegram from him and from the doctor last night both asking me to keep the wires busy."

"I see," he said understandingly, "I'll help you all I can in that respect. I'm afraid I've been rather remiss in the way of details, especially lately."

"You certainly have," she smiled.

"Well, what next?" he asked looking at his watch, and glancing uneasily toward the flapjacks that were being baked for them on the griddle in the window.

"Next," she said laughing, "I want a report every night of how much has been accomplished during the day. I'm afraid that may annoy you, but it can be very brief, just a thread to hang my report on. Mr. Fawcett was most insistent on that point in his final directions to me."

"You shall have it," said Duskin seriously. "I may have to use doughnut bags for stationery, but you shall have it. Third?"

Carol laughed.

"Third, I want you to assign me something to do. I'm here to work, and I want to know where to begin so that I may be efficient and not mess things."

"Work?" said Duskin puzzled. "Work? You? Why I thought you were my boss!"

Carol flushed embarrassedly.

"Oh, please," she said, "I'm afraid I've been quite disagreeable about things, but I'm not wanting to be. I only *represent* your boss, you know. I'm here to work, to do anything that can further the finishing of this building on time."

"Well, that's very good of you," he began. "But I don't quite see what you could do. You're neither a carpenter, a plumber, an electrician, a stone mason nor a plasterer—"

"No," laughed Carol, "although I think I could help out with any one of them in an emergency if someone showed me how. I'm ready to fill in anywhere. But in the meantime, I *am* a stenographer and secretary, and I can attack that mess on your desk in the office and get some of those letters off your conscience. I should think that might help a little."

"It would," said Duskin fervently. "It certainly would. Would you be willing to do that for me? I'm not keen on letter writing, not with all this other stuff on my hands. People are so blamed insistent that they shall know everything when I've got all I can do to do the thing without telling them about it. Also, people don't keep their promises. They don't send things when they say they will, and they hold me up at every turn. Why I have to waste at least two hours of every day bawling out people over the telephone."

"I was figuring to take that off your hands, too," smiled Carol. "They say I'm quite effective in that line at home."

"Good!" said Duskin smiling. "I see day dawning!" He looked at his watch again, and took his last hot cake.

"Can't I do your ordering, too?" she asked in a businesslike tone.

"I'm afraid not," he said doubtfully. "That would entail your being down there on the job at all hours, and it's no fit place for a woman."

"I expect to be there at all hours," said Carol quietly. "It's what I came for, and if it isn't a fit place I'll make it so; don't worry about me. Just send down your orders and I'll attend to them. That's been my business for quite a while you know."

"But—" said Duskin.

"If you please, no buts. You said I represented your boss and this is what he wants me to do."

"Very well, I submit," said Duskin. "And now I want to ask one thing of you?"

"Surely," said Carol brightly, "I will if I can."

"You *must!*" said Duskin. "It's important. You must be *very careful* about it. When I get time I'll explain more fully, but in the meantime I want to ask you to have as little to do with Schlessinger or any of his friends as possible. Don't put yourself in a position where you will be under obligation to them, and don't trust yourself alone *anywhere* with them. I may seem foolish, but I have my reasons. And if I were you I would be careful how I made friends. I'm glad you have some acquaintances here for that reason. You said you knew them well? These people you're going to dinner with tonight?"

"Why, no," said Carol, "not personally, but they are friends of Mrs. Fawcett."

"Which Mrs. Fawcett, Chicago or New York?" he asked sharply.

"New York."

"Oh, well, they're probably all right then. *Fred* Fawcett's wife runs around with a pretty fast crowd. Well, I hope you won't have too hard a time, and you'll be careful, won't you? Don't be too ready to trust strangers."

He suddenly looked down at her and laughed.

"I guess you won't," and they both remembered how he had told her yesterday that she did not trust him.

"By the way," he said as he slipped off his high stool and helped her down, "what's become of Delaplaine? Where does he get off in this scheme of things."

"He gets off," said Carol her cheeks flaming.

"I see. But how? Did you dismiss him?"

Carol hesitated, then she lifted honest humiliated eyes.

"No, he dismissed himself!"

Duskin laughed, a merry twinkle in his eyes.

"Good old Delaplaine. I knew he wouldn't come if he understood, but I'm sorry *you* didn't do it. I hoped that perhaps you had come to have a little more confidence in me of yourself. Just in the nature of things."

"I have."

"You would, naturally after talking with Delaplaine. He's that way. I can't help it."

"But I have," persisted Carol, "of myself."

He looked at her wistfully.

"I hope someday that'll really be true," he said earnestly. Then he opened the door for her and they were out in the street once more.

"I must hurry," he said with another glance at his watch, "I had a phone call in for half past, long distance. Excuse me, won't you? Come down tomorrow afternoon about two, and maybe I'll have been able to straighten out my desk before that and have some letters for you to write."

"But I'm coming along now," she said firmly. "I can straighten out that desk much quicker and better than you can. It's my business. You needn't worry lest I'll read any of your private correspondence. I'm not that kind."

"Help yourself," he laughed. "I haven't had any time for private correspondence for a year. It seems awful for me to let you attack that mess in my office, but go to it if that's what you want. Sorry I can't help you."

He was up the steps and at the telephone which was wildly ringing as he reached it and was saying, "Duskin at the phone." A few words of conversation, a quick, "Send it by fast express this afternoon. If it doesn't reach me by tomorrow morning the deal's all off. Good-bye."

Carol had lingered in the hall till he was through, and when he dashed by her to give some directions to the men at work on the elevator he did not seem to see her. Perhaps he had already forgotten her. Strange she had ever thought that he was lazy and indifferent to his job. How wrong she had been.

She went into the office, and took stock of the situation. Then she went to the telephone and called up a typewriter agency ordering a machine sent down to the building at once for immediate use. After a quick investigation of the supply of stationery in the desk drawers she looked up a stationer and ordered some paper, pencils, erasers, and a few other supplies. Then she took off her hat and set to work.

She had just gathered off the first layer of papers from the desk when a shadow loomed in the doorway, stealthily, and did not pass on like the other shadows that came and went. Looking up she saw Schlessinger standing there watching her with fond foxy eyes and a smile!

Chapter 12

Carol experienced a sudden feeling of fright when she saw who it was. Yet there were plenty of people about and of course her feeling was foolish. Still there had been something sinister in Duskin's warning.

"So, I have found you at last!" said Schlessinger with an intimacy in his tone which she resented.

"Oh, Mr. Schlessinger, were you looking for me?" she asked in her most businesslike tone. "Did you get the letter from the office you said you were expecting?"

"Why, no, I'm not sure whether one came or not," said Schlessinger indifferently. "It wasn't about that. I was looking for you to take you to lunch, little girl! How sweet you are looking today. Girls of today know how to look sweet always, don't they?"

Carol flushed angrily, but decided to ignore his compliments:

"It is impossible for me to take time for social engagements, Mr. Schlessinger. I'm sorry if you have not received your answer from the office. They are probably very busy. With Mr. Fawcett and me both away it makes the office a little short you know, and there is a lot to do. I'll wire them to forward your reply by telegraph if you are in haste."

"Oh, not at all, not at all. There's no haste whatever. But why are you so shy of social engagements, little girl? I want you to meet some of my friends. It isn't every day we have a visitor to our little old city so distinguished both for her beauty and her cleverness!"

"Excuse me, Mr. Schlessinger. I would rather you wouldn't

talk like that. I am here for business and nothing else, and have no desire for social engagements."

"But you are going out to dinner tonight with Mrs. Arthwait."

Suddenly with relief she saw that Duskin was standing in the doorway just behind Schlessinger, glaring at his back.

"Now, Schlessinger," he fairly roared, "if you will follow me I will show you what arrangements we are making for the lights in your private office. Just step this way quickly please. The lift is about to go up, and the men have had to stop working until it is out of the way."

Schlessinger turned sharply, almost angrily, and his aplomb disappeared as soundlessly as the gas goes out of a toy balloon.

"Oh, Duskin! That you? Why such haste? Oh—Ah—Well—I'll see you in a few minutes, Miss Berkley," and he bowed himself after the frowning Duskin.

Carol Berkley was not in the office when Schlessinger came down a few minutes later, assiduously attended by Duskin. Schlessinger went prowling around every room, and even insisted on going down to the cellar on some trifling excuse or other, wasting a good half hour of Duskin's time keeping tab on him, but he could not find any trace of the secretary. She had taken her hat and fled as soon as the lift was up out of sight, and was even then biding her time in a telephone booth of the drugstore across the way, where she could watch the door and yet be hidden from the street.

It was not until Schlessinger's car had turned the corner and was out of sight that she came out of her hiding, and went back to her work in the office. It certainly was going to be strenuous work being secretary for Duskin in that building.

But she had the letters in neatly assorted piles, duly strapped with rubber bands, labeled, and put away in the drawers before she left the building at half past six. She was all ready to go to work bright and early the next morning, and she decided on the way back to the hotel that she would ask Duskin to see that there was a lock and key for the door of the office before another day passed. She simply could not work if she had to keep a weather eye out for Schlessinger and his sort all the time.

She would rather have remained at the office that evening and if she had not promised to go to dinner with Mrs. Arthwait she would have risked another meal at the hot dog shop and got a lot of letters answered for Duskin to sign next day.

She had telephoned the hotel to get in touch with the Arthwaits if possible and give them a message that she would not be able to dine with them, but she had utterly failed to locate them, and there seemed nothing to be done at that hour but to keep her engagement.

She took a taxi back to the hotel knowing that she would have all she could do to get ready before the hour set, which was half past seven.

She hesitated what to wear for she had no idea where they were going but finally decided on the black dress once more. She wanted to keep her character of a businesswoman and not look too festive, although she was longing to try out the little blue chiffon that her mother had finished only two or three days ago, and that looked like a dream as it hung in the closet. But the memory of Paisley Arthwait's chinless face and affected waxed moustache made her firm. She did not want to seem to dress up for him.

She looked very lovely however in the severe lines of the black frock, and her little black hat. She was just fastening the silver rose on her shoulder more securely when the telephone buzzed and word came that the Arthwait car was awaiting her pleasure.

She hurried down, wishing the evening were over. She wanted

to get a good sleep tonight, to be ready for work early in the morning. If it were at all possible she would beg to be excused as soon as dinner was over, and ask to be taken back to the hotel. Of course she must be polite however if she found they had bought tickets for something. She would probably have to see the whole thing through on Mrs. Fawcett's account. Although, why should Mrs. Fawcett care whether her husband's secretary went with one of her old schoolmates or not? There really was no obligation.

She found young Paisley standing by the desk awaiting her.

"The car is just out here," he said, leading her toward the door. She came out to the entrance to find a handsome limousine drawn up in the shadow at one side. Paisley opened the door and she stepped in expecting to find Mrs. Arthwait. Paisley slammed the door shut and hurried around to the other side of the car, and when Carol looked she saw that she was seated in the front seat, with Paisley getting in beside her, and no one else in the backseat.

"Why, where is your mother?" she asked, startled.

"Oh, that's so," he replied, "I forgot to explain, didn't I? Why, Mother—" just then he got in a particularly congested bit of traffic, and for a moment or two, had all he could do to extricate himself, and Carol had a few thrills on her own account as the car nearly collided with two others, escaping by a hairsbreadth.

"Pardon me," he resumed, as they sped around a corner into a quieter street, "where was I? Oh, yes, Mother has been having a fierce time today. She is subject to terrific headaches, and worse luck one came on today. She's been doctoring up all day, tried all her usual remedies, but though the severe pain has left her, she's as weak as a rag, and not fit to sit up, much less eat any dinner. She's awfully sorry to miss it, but she said to tell you she'd go next time, and we must enjoy it for her too."

"Oh, but—really—" gasped Carol sitting up straight in her seat and speaking earnestly. "Won't you please turn back and let us wait until your mother is better? I couldn't think of going without her, and I am very tired myself."

"Oh, no indeedy!" refused the young man laughing, and stepping on the gas. "Mother wouldn't forgive me if I let you do that. Besides, our table is engaged and everything arranged for."

"Well, but," said Carol looking wildly about her and wishing she could jump out, "couldn't you call up and cancel the reservation? I really would be much happier to wait till your mother can go along. Besides, I've been trying to get you on the telephone all the afternoon to tell you that I was afraid I should have to put it off on account of other things that have come up. It was only because I failed to get you up to the last minute that I hurriedly got ready to go. It really would be much more convenient to me if you would take me back and let me go some other evening."

"Nothing doing!" grinned the young man fiendishly, and stepped on the gas still harder. "Aw, you needn't worry if it's chaperones you're thinking about. There'll be plenty of Mother's friends out there. I'll ring in one of them if you insist, though Mother thought we'd have a much better time by ourselves, and nobody bothers about chapys anymore."

Carol said nothing. She was trying to think of a way out of it, and a sudden memory of Duskin's warning, and Schlessinger's last sentence: "You're going out to dinner with Mrs. Arthwait," came to her. She had forgotten it in her busy afternoon. How did Schlessinger happen to know about the dinner? Was he a friend of the Arthwaits? Her heart began to beat rapidly. It was then that she had for the first time a sudden memory of Schlessinger's walking over toward the big couch to speak to someone, as she was being carried up in the elevator the night before. Was that only the night before? So many things had happened since then. Yes, and hadn't those same two people sat on that couch as

Schlessinger first approached her? A purple dress, and white hair!

But it was no use thinking things like this now. She must either coax this youth to take her back, or make the best of it.

"I really would be obliged to you if you would take me back," she said gravely.

"Aw, now, be a good sport," he laughed. "I'll show you a good time all right, just as good as if the old dame had gone along. Besides, we're almost there now."

Carol glanced out and saw that they were out in the country, speeding along at a terrific rate. The car careened from one side to the other whenever they struck a rough bit of road, and the few lighted dwellings along the way were far between and seemed to shoot by like comets. Even if she could force him to let her out here, what could she do? She would not know how to get back alone.

"Where are we going?" she asked anxiously.

"Oh, out to a dandy place where they have great eats! Make a specialty of chicken and waffles, and things like that. Have wonderful mushrooms too; steak and mushrooms to make your mouth water! People come from Chicago down here to get their steak and mushroom dinners. Greatest ever. Plenty to drink too. Get anything you want. Have a cigarette?"

He offered her a gold cigarette case.

"No thank you," she declined coldly, "I don't smoke."

"Why not?" he asked unabashed. "All the girls doing it. Better learn tonight. No time like the present."

"Thank you, I don't care to!" Carol's tone was freezing. She began to feel more and more uncomfortable. She decided that she would demand to be taken home immediately after dinner. She wished with all her heart that she had never come. Here again was another of her fatal mistakes. Oh, why had she been sent to this terrible city! What would her mother say if she could see her now, speeding along through the night to nobody knew where with a stranger who talked in a tongue that belonged to another world than hers.

But Paisley did not seem to be troubled by the coldness of her tone. He drove wildly on, turning now and then a corner on two wheels it seemed, dashing down another road, and over to a second highway, barely escaping collision with an oncoming truck, and rattling gaily on again as if it had been nothing.

"Saw a great smashup here the other night," he announced merrily. "Girl half stewed couldn't work her brakes, and ran into a milk truck. Gosh it was great! The milk swashed all over, and the girl was all blood, glass broke in her windshield, you know. Fella with her was dead to the world and just lay in the ditch and didn't say a thing! Gosh it was funny!"

"Why was it funny!" asked Carol in a still, terrible voice, shrinking away from him with a shudder. What kind of a youth was this, anyway?

"Why? Oh, it was a scream! There was milk everywhere, and the girl's hat was all blood, and her makeup was all milk."

"I wish you would take me home," said Carol suddenly sitting up very straight and determined, "I don't feel at all well. I must get back at once."

"You'll be all right when we get there," asserted the youth easily. "Need a little fresh air. Here, I'll open that window beside you," and he leaned intimately across her and wound down the sash.

Carol shrank still farther into the cushion, and looked wildly out at the darkness rushing by, wishing she dared jump out.

"Only a mile ahead now. Feel any better? Like to lie down? Put your head on my shoulder," he suggested amiably. "I don't mind. Do you good to rest a little. You've been working too hard I guess. All work and no play. We're going to play tonight, get me.

There, put your head down," and he attempted to draw her over to his shoulder with his one free hand.

"Oh, no thank you," said Carol briskly, sitting up very straight and stiff. "I'll just put my face close to the window and get the air. It is a little close tonight. I'll be all right now I think."

She was terribly frightened and sat away from him as far as she could, but it was an immense relief when they rushed out of a wooded stretch into the open and saw a burst of light ahead.

"Here we are, all okay," announced her escort gaily. "Now, aren't you glad you've come?"

Carol made out a long low house with a porch across its whole front, garishly picked out in red and yellow electric bulbs, and set in a grove of tall poplars. The many windows behind the lights were dark, however, with closely drawn shades. Many cars were parked about, and the whole atmosphere seemed permeated with an air of giddy mystery. She cast an anxious eye about the landscape and there seemed nothing else in sight but hills and valleys as far as she could see. A great white moon had suddenly come out from behind a bank of clouds and illuminated the world. It seemed the loneliest spot that she had ever seen.

Paisley parked his car in the line with other noble machines, and helped her out. She was glad to get on solid ground again, no matter where she was, but she went up the steps from the terrace, to this gaudy piazza with its many cretonned rockers and settees, and not a soul in sight, with a great misgiving. What kind of a place was this to which she had come?

She was not a girl given to going about much to cafés and roof gardens. She had not time nor money nor yet inclination for such things. But instinct taught her that here was a place about which there was something peculiar, and she wished sincerely that she were back in the hotel.

However, there seemed nothing to do but follow her escort. She could not very well turn and run away from him down the road, and if she did she wouldn't be able to get very far from Paisley before he could catch her, for her knees were weak with fright, and she must be miles and miles from anywhere.

When she got inside the place she was not much reassured. There was the same garishness of red and yellow about the room, and the place was blue with smoke, and giddy with jazz. Strange, she had not seemed to notice the music until the door opened. The walls must be very thick. It seemed to be an old stone farm-house extended and made over.

But there were people there in plenty, dressed more garishly than the rooms, and their voices were noisy and unrestrained.

Paisley led her to a table, one of the few unoccupied ones, and she sat down weakly and looked about her while Paisley raised his voice and called greetings to various tables far and near and made himself generally conspicuous.

Carol had never been in such an atmosphere before and she hated it. She was not one to snatch at any experience for once just to get an experience. She felt disgusted.

There was a table just to the right of theirs where liquor was flowing freely, and the six people who occupied it must have been there for some time, and imbibed a great many drinks, for they were very much beside themselves, and had begun to address their conversation to the general public. As Carol sat down, one of the men turned bleary eyes toward her and began to speak to her in loud fulsome terms.

"Well, sweetie, where'd you come from? Look at those eyes. Boys, I'm smitten!"

Carol turned sharply away and looked to her weak-chinned escort for protection, but he only grinned.

"Ben Wiley," he said. "Don't mind him. He's a good sport but he's stewed tonight, really stewed he is—I'll introduce you by and by when the dancing begins."

"Don't!" said Carol sharply. "I shouldn't care to know him."

"Aw, he's all right!" said Paisley, comfortably. "Got a fifteen-thousand-dollar car that's a beaut. His uncle bought it for him, and he killed a kid the first day he drove it. Say, what'll you have to drink?"

"Coffee!" said Carol quickly. "Very hot." She shuddered and drew her silk coat about her neck. Would she ever get out of this terrible place?

Behind her the young man of the convivial nature was protesting loudly against his comrades who were trying to hush the song he had begun to sing, looking pointedly and stupidly at Carol as he sang:

> "Oh, I'd like to have a little sweetheart,
> Just like youoooo!"

He had evidently attempted to point the climax by a tap on Carol's shoulder, for she heard his voice suddenly approach her ear, and then his comrades drew him back and murmured something in his ear.

"What's that?" he shouted. "Put me out? Why they can't put me outta here. Why, don't you know I could buy two of these places and put 'em in my pocket? Lemme alone! I like that new girl. I'm goin' over an' talk to her. Who's that brought her? Paiz? Hello, Paiz, whose's yer friend? Len' her to me awhile?"

Carol suddenly arose from her chair and spoke to Arthwait in a tense tone.

"I can't sit here any longer. Take me to another table or let us get out of here! I'm not used to being insulted!"

"Aw, he's just stewed," exclaimed Paisley rising and trying to detain her, "everybody understands him. Sit down, Carol. Your name's Carol I know. Mother saw it on a telegram they had at the desk for you. Don't let's be formal. You call me Paisley. Sit down. You have to. There isn't any other place and our order's coming now. Besides, a friend of yours is coming who wants to have a nice little talk with you."

"I'm going outside," said Carol in new terror. "I'll wait for you in the car."

"No use, Carol!" said Arthwait with a leer, "they keep these doors locked fer fear of a raid. You couldn't get out unless I went with you. You don't know the password. Didn't you see me use my key when I came in? Sit down, Carol, and be a good sport. You needn't get excited. The lights all go out if anybody comes nosing around."

And then openly she saw him give a slow deliberate wink toward the table where his drunken friend sat.

Too frightened to speak, too weak to stand, Carol sank into the chair once more, white to the lips.

The food was brought and placed before them but she did not look at it. Liquor was poured for her, but she refused it. She was afraid even to sip the coffee which she had ordered. And suddenly as she stared blindly across the room trying to think what she could do, trying to find a face she thought she could trust, someone to whom she might appeal for assistance, she became aware of Schlessinger's fox face, smiling at her above the crowd. Schlessinger, the only man she knew in the assemblage and he a fox! Oh, what a fool she had been!

She saw it now, a scheme, to take her unawares, and perhaps try to bribe her to help them in their devilment, force her to give up information, turn her against Duskin again! Oh, why had she not told Duskin about that conversation she had heard in New

York between Schlessinger and Blintz, and used the evidence she had against them before it was too late. Could it be possible that they knew she had heard them? Oh, was she crazy to think such things? Perhaps Paisley Arthwait and his mother were just a couple of fools who really meant to give her a pleasant evening and chose this kind of thing because they liked it. Doubtless she was all upset over nothing. And yet, Schlessinger had known she was dining with the Arthwaits, and he was here himself!

As if to confirm her thought Paisley at that moment babbled forth:

"Why, there's Uncle Schless, now! Hello, old boy!" for Paisley had imbibed several glasses of liquid fire already, and he had chosen some that took quick effect. She noticed with horror that his tongue was already thick, and his eyes wore an unholy glitter. "Shess! Shess! Ole boy! Comme meer! Come see little Carol!"

And to her horror Schlessinger, smiling and licking his foxlike lips came quickly toward their table.

Carol rose up involuntarily, and looked this way and that in desperation. There seemed nowhere to flee, and Paisley rose too and called out to her, "Come, Caro. Come, Caro corn syrup, le's dance! Le's everybody dance."

At that instant, as she swayed away from Paisley there came a crash just behind her, and the lights went out in utter blackness. A strange low whistle went about the room, and people seemed silently scuttling in the dark, crawling away over broken glass.

There was cold air rushing in behind her and a voice low spoken, "Come, Carol!"

Someone had caught her about the waist and drawn her out of the way, into the cold air, but it was too late. There was no moon anymore and it was cold and dark, and everything was gone in terror.

Chapter 13

When Duskin came down to the office a little after seven he stopped with an exclamation of contentment and looked at his cleared up desk. It was empty, absolutely empty of the clutter that had been there for weeks.

A typewriter neatly covered with its rubber hood sat straight in the middle of the desk, and a mahogany letter tray occupied the right-hand corner.

He opened the right-hand top drawer and found an array of stationery and pencils and erasers and the like; investigated the other drawers and found the neat bundles of sorted letters each with its label, the top one bearing the admonition "IMPORTANT. Immediate."

He glanced at them and frowned to think he had forgotten them. She was a clever girl. She was going to be a great help. She had shown sense.

Then the city clock struck half past seven and he turned away, remembering that he had an important engagement to meet a man at eight and he must snatch some dinner and dress. He hurried over to the garage where he kept a cheap secondhand car which he had purchased when he first came to town, and drove as rapidly up the street as the traffic would allow.

His way led him past the hotel where Carol was staying and as he turned down the side street he noticed just ahead at the side entrance of the hotel a young man helping a girl into a big car. The girl looked like Miss Berkley. It must be about time for her to be going out. He wondered what her friends were like. He spurred up his faithful flivver to catch a glimpse if he could, and looking in the backseat found it empty. Could that be Miss Berkley in the front? The light did not shine on her face as he passed. Where had he seen that young man with the weak chin? Something unpleasant was connected with him. What was it?

The limousine lurched ahead and passed him, and again he failed to see the girl's face, yet something in the contour of shoulders and head reminded him of the girl from New York.

Caught in traffic almost together, he yet was where he could not see her face, nor identify her companion. His hands were so full steering his car out of the tangle that he could do very little looking.

Whoever the chinless young man was he was a rotten driver, and was taking terrible risks. He watched the big car go lurching on through traffic, till it whirled sharply away down another street, and then because he had a strong impression that the girl was now his new secretary, he turned his car and followed. After all it was going in the general direction he meant to take, and a minute or two wouldn't matter with him. He could still make his appointment.

The crazy driver ahead was holding his interest. Perhaps the man was drunk.

But when the big car turned sharply onto the pike and took to the country, Duskin followed only a mile or two further, and then turned back. He had decided that he was on a wild-goose chase, and he couldn't take time to keep it up any longer. He could scarcely have time to dress now. Dinner must wait until midnight perhaps. He had to meet his man.

He had gone perhaps half a mile back toward the city, pondering who that young man without a chin reminded him of, when he saw the lights of a big car coming toward him. It was a lonely road and the single big car with its arrogant lights was the more noticeable. As it drew nearer its lights were fairly blinding, but as it shot by a glimpse of a fox face and a long nose gleamed against the blackness of the back seat. Ah! That was the mayor's car! He had seen it many times! Schlessinger! Where was he going? Stay! It was with Schlessinger he had seen that young man! Wasn't he some relation to Schlessinger? Nephew? Where were they going? The *girl!*

Duskin turned his car so quickly he nearly lost control; then he throbbed off in pursuit of the mayor.

Not close on his heels, Oh, no! He kept too far behind to be studied by even the most detective of chauffeurs. He was only another jalopy, jogging along the highway, getting out of sight as often as possible, yet keeping the taillight of the mayor always in view.

Where *were* they going? And was he a fool? He was missing a most important appointment, one he had worked hard to get. It might mean delay in tomorrow's work. It might mean he would have to work hard to make up for the loss some other way. The man he was to meet had power with railroads and could command, and a freight car would come through in a night. There were materials that had not yet arrived, and would be needed in two more days. Yet Duskin kept his car's nose turned toward the taillight of the mayor.

And where was he going? A lonely road, and that sharp turn they were making ahead there, up through the woods? Wasn't there a roadhouse off here somewhere? Perhaps. He didn't pay much attention to things of that sort but he had overheard talk. Well, he was not surprised at the mayor, but—who was that girl? He must find out!

He didn't know he was such a blamed fool. But he had *got* to *find out.*

He almost halted at the wooded road. Suppose the car should go on all night? He could not follow indefinitely. Just then came the clear gleam of colored lights, and Duskin heard the cessation of the big car's engine, and drove his own into the bushes at the side of the road out of the way.

Stealthily he came up on foot. Yes, that last car was the mayor's, parked with its nose to the fence with the rest. He briefly swept the flashlight he always carried over its door and read the initials: "W. W. S." There was no further doubt. He went on to the next and identified it as the big car he had followed first from the hotel. He swept its door too with a bug of light, and there were the same initials. He was right, the young fellow must be a relative. It was one of Schlessinger's cars. From then on, his course was plain. He had to find out who that girl was! If Carol Berkley was not in that close shuttered, belighted house he might go on his way content and make the best he could of his time back, calling himself a fool all the way. But if she was—well—*if she was—!*

But it is no easy task to see into a room that has been purposely made proof against prying eyes, and Duskin stole twice around that building, carefully avoiding the back where the servants were handling freezers, and clattering dishes, before he discovered the one little spot where a drunken scuffle the night before had badly damaged the window shade. And that as it happened was across the room from the table where Carol and Paisley sat.

It was sometime before he got his eye properly adjusted to survey the room, and several minutes before he found what he was searching for. Yes, there she was, her delicate face and slim little black satin figure standing out like a flower among all those coarse, bedizened people. He caught his breath when he saw her, and watched, his brows lowering, his hands clenched.

It did not take him long to understand the situation. Indeed, Carol's attitude was plainly panic-stricken as any man might read, and though he could not hear what the man at the next table was saying he knew by the significant looks in that direction, and by the fright on the girl's face and the way she turned her eyes away piteously that it was nothing good.

He was about to spring away and try to force the door when he saw that look of horror come into her eyes anew, and his gaze followed hers and saw Schlessinger!

He waited only to number the windows that he might make no mistake, and then he crept stealthily about the house, pausing behind some shrubbery while some new arrivals came up on the porch. He tried to enter with them, but found the door shut in his face, and went on to the window which he knew was just behind Carol's table.

One moment he stood outside, calculating, looking back to count the windows again and make sure he had made no mistake, then he lifted the big whitewashed stone he had picked up from the edge of the drive, and smashed it through the glass, tearing away the dark lined curtain, and getting one glimpse of the room and its people before everything went black.

Blindly he groped for her where he had seen her, touched the softness of her gown, flashed his light on her face faintly and out again, and caught her in his arms.

There was blood on his hands where he had cut them climbing through the window, and blood on his face. He felt it trickle down and tossed his head to get it out of his eyes. The night was pitch black for the moon had gone into a storm cloud, and the air was breathless. All the red and yellow lights along the rim of the house had gone dead too. There was nothing stirring anywhere in the universe, but himself, and he hardly dared to breathe. The girl in his arms hung limp. He gathered her closer and stumbled across the drive and down into the woods to his car.

When he had put her in and started the car he reached out to touch her, fearful lest she had ceased to breathe, she lay so still, but she quivered away from his touch.

He pondered this as he hurried his car through the woods and back onto the highway again. He must make the best of his time. They might pursue him. At first perhaps they thought they were being raided, but they would find out—they would come after him—he must get the girl away.

When he had passed the woods and come a mile down the highway he took out his flashlight and turned it into the girl's face. He could not bear her stillness any longer. But when he looked he saw her eyes were open and full of fear.

She had not known who he was! Of course! He ought to have remembered that.

"Little girl," he said very gently, "I thought you were in trouble back there. Did I do right to bring you away?"

"Oh, is it you, Mr. Duskin? Oh, I am so glad," and he felt she was crying softly as she spoke.

"I have been—so—frightened!"

"Are you hurt?" he asked anxiously. "I'm afraid I was rather rough!"

"Oh, no, but I wouldn't mind if I was, I'm so thankful to be out of that terrible place! But I thought—I thought—you were Mr. Schlessinger!"

"You poor child!" said Duskin as he might have talked to a little girl of five, and his voice held a caress that she did not seem to mind.

Duskin forgot that he had had one fearful moment when he thought that perhaps this girl who had seemed so true and honorable had been one of the league against him too. How could he have harbored such a thought? But then, he had been through so much, and borne so many setbacks from this unscrupulous gang!

"It was all my fault!" she said earnestly. "But I didn't want to go with them. I tried to get word to Mrs. Arthwait that I couldn't go, but I could not get my message to her till it got so late I was ashamed to back out. And then her son came alone!"

"The creep! The miserable creep!" said Duskin under his breath.

"He got me into the car before he told me his mother was sick and couldn't go, and I *couldn't make* him take me back and wait until she could go. I tried my best."

"Look here!" said Duskin savagely, "don't you suppose I know it wasn't your fault? Don't you suppose I can see with a glance that you're not their kind? Oh, the dirty crooks! But I've got something on the mayor now that will make him clear out and let us alone for a while, I'm thinking. He won't want it known that he went to a place like that. Perhaps we can work in peace for a little while till he thinks up a new way to torment us."

"Oh!" she said suddenly, her voice full of eagerness. "We've got more than that on him. I ought to have told you long ago! What a fool I have been not to trust you!"

And then she began at the beginning and told him all about the conversation she had overheard between Schlessinger and Blintz back in the New York office.

"And you say you have the full notes of all that?" he asked eagerly.

"Every word."

"Then we'll fix the old fox for a fact! But we'll finish the building first and wait for Fawcett if possible. Say, you are great! You've pulled off the biggest thing you could have done when you took down that conversation! That certainly was clever of you. I've had a hunch all along that we were going to have trouble with those two birds at the end. They'll have something else up their sleeves to spring on us at the last minute or I'll miss my guess. But this finishes that. They can't pull anything in the face of that evidence! I could shout for joy! But say—are *you* all right?"

He turned the flashlight full on her face once more, and by its reflection she saw his face.

"Yes, but you are not!" she cried. "Why, there's blood on your face, Mr. Duskin, and on your hands. It's running down. Let me tie it up."

"No, I'm quite all right," said Duskin with a sudden light of delirious joy in his eyes. To have her speak to him in that voice went quite to his head. What was the matter with him? He ought to have eaten his dinner. He never before had a girl's sympathy affect him like that!

"It's just a little cut in my hand, from the glass," he explained, and felt as if he were shouting it from the hilltops. Why did he feel so glad? It was out of all proportion.

"I'm going to tie it up!" said Carol firmly, bringing out a soft handkerchief and dabbing at his hurt hand.

He stopped the car and suffered her to tie up his hand.

"You're very kind," he said in a tone that was almost embarrassed. "That's the way my mother used to do when I was a little kid."

"Kind?" said Carol, "when you saved my life!"

"Oh, no, I don't anticipate they would have gone as far as that," he said. "But I do think they intended to detain you awhile to get what information they could out of you. Very likely their plan was to force you to fire me."

"Oh, do you really think that?" she said appalled. "Do you think it really was intentional?"

"I should say I did," he answered vehemently. "Didn't you know you were riding in one of Schlessinger's cars? I made sure of that before I went to look in the house."

"Oh, mercy!" said Carol pausing in her bandaging to look up in horror. "How terrible! I was frightened enough as it was, but if I had known that I certainly would have jumped out!"

"Well, that's not so good either," he smiled down at her. "But come, that's enough. I must get you out of this. They might track us down even now. If they thought they could they would, you know. It would be lovely for them if they could take me too; it would be so much velvet. If they could just get me back to that roadhouse and then spread a story that I had been out there, and broadcast it back to Fawcett. Don't you see what we'd have been up against?"

"Oh, and to think I did it! What a fool I have been! You must have thought—well—all sorts of things about me."

"Well, to tell you the truth I didn't know what to think at first. When I saw you in that car, or thought I did, I wasn't positive it was you, with that fool of an Arthwait. No woman about either. You had led me to suppose it was a woman who had invited you. That troubled me some, although I realized you might have changed your plans afterwards. You were not obliged to tell me everything of course. Still, it was an ugly thought. I followed you to prove to myself that it wasn't you, and then when I found it was I knew I must get you out somehow, if only to find out what it was all about."

"You have been wonderful," she said humbly. "I feel as if I can never thank you, and never apologize sufficiently."

"For what?" he asked.

She was still a minute.

"Well, for distrusting you in the first place and then for getting you into all this and wasting more of your time. Didn't I hear you making an appointment over the phone this afternoon to meet a man at eight o'clock? You've missed that, haven't you? And I heard you say it was very important."

"You were more important," he said quickly. "Suppose I had succeeded in getting all the freight cars through I wanted, and then had found you were gone, kidnapped, and I had to spend the rest of my time hunting you?"

"I'm beginning to be convinced that you would be much better off without me," said Carol still more humbly. "I have been an awful fool, and you have been marvelous!"

"Look here," said Duskin, "you and I just haven't understood each other, that was all. When we get time we'll sit down and explain a lot of things. Until then we'll have to take each other on trust. We've got a big work to do, and it will help a lot if we do teamwork. How about it, are you willing to trust me that far?"

"I'm certainly willing to trust you entirely, and I'll begin by asking you if there isn't still time for you to catch that man you were to see? If you put me down here on the edge of the city where I can take a trolley back to the hotel, and you drive hard, couldn't you perhaps get him yet? I can't bear to think I've kept you from that appointment. If you would stop at a drugstore and telephone, say you had to help somebody out of trouble, wouldn't he perhaps wait till you got there?"

"I shall not drop you out anywhere, be assured of that," he said decidedly, "but if you don't mind sitting in the car I might take the chance and drive around that way. Are you sure you wouldn't mind?"

"It would relieve me greatly," she said eagerly, "and won't you telephone?"

"I will," he said. "That's a good suggestion."

He drew up in front of a little country drugstore.

"I shan't be gone but a minute, and you are all safe here in the bright light. Plenty of people about, if any of those crooks come hunting you."

"I'm not afraid," she smiled, "but I'd advise you to ask the druggist to let you wash your face before you go calling."

He grinned.

"Thank you, I'll do that also."

She watched him go into the telephone booth, and then disappear into the back of the store. But he was gone only a few minutes.

"It's all right," he said jumping into the car, "he says he'll wait till I get there. And I got the druggist to put some stuff on my cuts so I don't look quite so disreputable. Now, if you don't mind going fast, I promised him I'd be there in ten minutes."

"I love to go fast."

There was no chance to talk as the car thundered through the city streets, and Carol had time to sit back in the hard little seat and think how much pleasanter this ride was than the one she had taken an hour before in the expensive limousine.

They came to the house before the ten minutes were up, and Duskin left her in the car and sprang up the steps. She watched him as he stood there under the bright light of the front door, a splendid figure, even in his rough clothes and old panama hat. His trousers might be bagged at the knees perhaps, from too much kneeling down on the floor with the pliers to pull up electric wires, but he had the ease and grace of one born to the purple. He could look his man in the eye and make him forget what he had on. And straightway she began to wonder that she had not known it all along. And then again she said: "What a fool, what a terrible fool I have been! Was I always a fool? Will I always stay a fool? I have made a worse mistake every day I have been here. Perhaps I ought to go home!"

But strangely enough she suddenly realized that she did not want to go home. She wanted to stay and see the whole thing through.

He did not stay long, and he came back with a spring in his step.

"It's all right," he said and he threw in the clutch. "That man's a prince. I wish I'd gone to him before. He says he'll see us through, and if anybody attempts to sidetrack our cars, and they don't come through on the dot, we're to phone him and he'll give it personal attention. He says he knew my father in college. That's what it is to have a father!"

"You're sure he isn't a relative of the mayor's?" asked Carol meekly.

"Quite sure," he laughed. "I've heard my mother speak of him. He's all right. By the way, did you eat anything in that dump out there?"

"No," said Carol with a shudder. "I was too frightened, and there was too much wine about. I didn't want to eat. I kept thinking of your warning. You know it never entered my head that there was anything wrong with my taking dinner with those people, they had been so kind the night before, although I was bored to death with them. But they were so insistent I thought I ought to go."

"Forget them," said Duskin, "let's have a good time. I'm starved, aren't you? Hot dogs and flannel cakes are all right in their place but they don't last forever. Let's have a square meal."

He took her to a quiet place where they could have a table in a secluded corner, and he ordered steak and lyonnaise potatoes, new peas, lima beans, and corn, and they had a merry time eating it. Carol began to feel as if she had known Duskin always, and wondered that she had ever misunderstood him.

"Now," said he when they had finished a delectable ice disguised in whipped cream and fruits, and had merrily divided the last piece of cake and eaten every crumb of it, "are you dead tired? How would you like to come over to the building and see the new automatic fire extinguisher? The boys were unpacking it when I left. It's a very interesting piece of machinery. They're going to install it tomorrow."

"I'd love it," said Carol. "How I wish I had accepted your offer to show me over the building tonight, and called off that awful dinner. Then you wouldn't have had all this trouble. Only—" she paused, and her cheeks grew rosy.

"Only what?" he asked watching her with keen eyes.

"Well, we might not have understood—that is you—I—"

"You mean we might not have understood each other so well? You mean we might not have *trusted* each other, is that it?"

Her eyes met his, and she gave him a grave, sweet "Yes."

"Then I'm glad it happened," he said and gave her one of his rare smiles.

"Then come," he said, "we'll begin your education in construction, although we won't get far tonight now. It's quarter to ten and you ought to get to resting pretty soon."

"Oh, I'm not at all tired anymore," declared Carol.

As she climbed back into the car she had a sense of relief and a feeling of protection about it. It was good to be protected and by a strong man like this one. How he had given her the sense that he was powerful, that he was about her as a wall! It was her high tension this evening of course. She had never felt that she wanted protection. She had always rather rejoiced in her independence heretofore.

They drove to the building, and found Charlie and Roddy and their gangs like so many boys with a new toy. They had unpacked the shining parts and were putting them together.

They did not look up when Duskin brought the girl up in the lift. They kept their eyes averted, and the man Charlie studied his beloved boss furtively. For some reason he saw Duskin had changed his tactics. Was the boss going to fall for that girl?

Yet the girl had changed her tactics too. She no longer said insolent things to the boss. She asked him questions humbly as a little child. She exclaimed with pleasure over the perfect fittings and the rapidity with which they had done the work on the fixtures since her last trip to the upper floors, and she gave respectful attention to all the boss had to say. Was this just one more trick of a dirty little crook, or had she learned her onions? Charlie wasn't sure, and he was taking no chances. But in everything he followed the lead of Duskin. What Duskin said, went with him every time.

Duskin led the girl about the whole floor where she had arrived uninvited for her first interview with him. He showed her what had been done since the day before yesterday, explaining in detail what the first electricians had done, or rather left undone, which made it necessary to do a lot of the work over again. She heard about the wholesale dismissal of the first gang and how Duskin had taken the train for Chicago to hunt up his old gang of friends upon whom he knew he could depend. She gathered that there was some bond between them closer than between workmen and boss, closer even than friends, more like brothers who had suffered together and loved one another. And somehow the words she had overheard the night before about herself lost their sting. Perhaps they were justified in suspecting everyone until he was proved trustworthy.

To her astonishment the whistles were blowing for midnight before they turned to go downstairs. The men said good-night respectfully, and Charlie in a manner more formal than he was wont to use toward Duskin informed him that they would all be there when he came back.

"Do they never sleep?" asked Carol.

"Not if they think I'll be waking," he smiled. "We've got some work yet to do tonight and they won't let me stay alone and do it."

"Put me on the trolley then," she pleaded. "You must not take any more time for me tonight. I feel condemned."

But he would not leave her until he saw her to the door of the hotel.

The newsboys were crying the first edition of the morning paper as he helped her out of the car and walked with her to the door.

"All about the mayor's trip to the Canadian Rockies!" yelled a little urchin in their ears.

"Ah?" said Duskin turning sharply, "what have we here? Paper, kid!"

He bought one and they stepped within the entrance to look at it.

Duskin ran his finger down the columns of the front page:

"Ah, here we have it! Listen," he said:

"Mayor Schlessinger with a couple of friends, started early yesterday morning for a fishing trip through the Canadian Rockies. He expects to be gone two or three weeks, and will later be joined by his wife, his sister, and nephew who will travel through California with him."

"And so," said Duskin, "the noble mayor has provided himself with an alibi. Rapid work. Early *yesterday morning!* Neat, that! But now perhaps we can get something done."

When Carol got up to her room once more, she opened her Bible and read over thoughtfully that verse about the companionship of fools, and then she read on till she came to another startling verse: "Seest thou a man, wise in his own conceit? There is more hope of a fool than of him." She bowed her head and gave a little moan of humiliation. How that Bible cut into one's very soul! How it read one to the core! That was what she had been—wise in her own conceit! And if it had not been for Duskin where would she be now? Oh, what a fool she had been! How could she ever learn wisdom?

Then, as if to answer her, a breath of air came in the open window and turned the pages, and her eyes fell on these words: "The fear of the Lord is the beginning of wisdom: and the knowledge of the holy is understanding." Turning, with a look of surrender, she dropped upon her knees and prayed: "Oh Lord, teach me Thy wisdom! Help me to know Thee."

And she had thought that Proverbs was impersonal!

Chapter 14

The work of straightening out Duskin's office progressed rapidly. Carol was in her place at eight o'clock in the morning clicking away busily at the typewriter, but she saw nothing of Duskin until half past eleven when he came in to telephone.

He flashed a smile at her, and asked if she felt all right and then snapped a message into the telephone.

"There are a lot of letters waiting for your signature," she said as he turned to go out.

"They'll have to wait," he said crisply. "This is an awful morning. I'm not sure I can keep my appointment with you this afternoon. I may have to run up to Chicago. Something's gone wrong with a consignment of trim that was ordered two weeks ago. We've got to have it by Monday if I have to hire a truck and drive it down myself."

He vanished and she went on working. At two she went out to the hot-dog shop, sat on a stool and ate sausages and flapjacks and came back to work. Some of the important letters she signed "FAWCETT CONSTRUCTION COMPANY" per C. W. Berkley and posted them. The big building was silent, except for Bill shambling to the front door occasionally. But there was plenty to do so she went back to work again.

At five she laid aside the company papers and wrote a long letter to Mr. Fawcett, supplementing the various telegrams she had sent. She found herself speaking of the young construction engineer in the highest terms, and paused to wonder how her viewpoint had changed in one evening.

At six Charlie presented himself, speckless as to attire, and announced that the boss asked him to come and take her to her hotel. The boss had found he had to go to Chicago.

Carol told Charlie it was wholly unnecessary for him to take her to the hotel, that she had a few more letters to write, and would take a taxi back when she was through.

"That's all right," said Charlie, "I'll wait in the hall till you're ready."

"That's very kind of you," said Carol, "but it really isn't necessary. I'm used to going about alone."

"It's the boss's orders," said Charlie as if that settled it, and looking at the red-haired Scotchman she seemed to see the same determination in the set lips and the firm chin that sat upon his friend and superior's face.

Carol laughed.

"Then I suppose I'll have to obey," she said amusedly. "What time do you expect him back?"

"Can't say," said Charlie. "He left about 'leven-thirty. Took a big truck. He oughtta got there before six o'clock, maybe five. Don't know how long it would take 'em to load up. Might be back by midnight, might take till morning! 'Cording if he don't have engine trouble."

"He didn't go alone, did he?" she asked anxiously. "It's much more important that he should be attended than that I should."

The man Charlie flickered her a wise eye and nodded.

"He wanted to," he admitted, "but we didn't see it. Roddy and Ted went along. They each took a couppla guns, also, but the boss wasn't wise to it. He's pretty good at taking care of himself, but we weren't running any risks."

"I'm glad you didn't," said Carol getting up and beginning to put on her hat. "But I'm wondering how he's going to get his material. It's Saturday afternoon. Will the place be open?"

"You bet it will! The boss got 'em on the wire and told 'em

where to get off." Charlie was warming to the lady boss. She seemed to be learning all her vegetables quickly.

"But ought we to leave the building alone, with just Bill?" inquired Carol as she slipped her papers into the desk and locked the drawers. "I know Mr. Duskin is rather particular about that."

"Building's all right," asserted Charlie. "Pete and Sam and three of Roddy's men are up on top. They're comin' down and stick around while I'm gone, and we calculate to remain parked here all night."

"That's fine," said Carol appreciatively. "Couldn't I help too? I'll stay here now while you go out to dinner."

"Thanks, awfully, but we got our orders. Dinner's coming in relays tonight. Couple of us go out and bring back grub for the rest."

"Well, I see we are all in good hands," smiled Carol following him down the steps to the old flivver, and wondering at herself for so soon losing her feeling against these men who had called her a dirty little crook.

When Charlie left her at the hotel he further announced:

"The boss said he wished you'd stay where you are till he gets back. He didn't have time to write you a note, so I said I'd tell ya. He said he might wantta call ya up, and it would save time."

"I'll stay," she said smilingly. "Let me know if anything happens. You know I'm interested, and I'll be glad to help in any way."

Charlie grinned.

"You're all right, little lady," he said heartily, "I'll do that little thing if we get in any jams. Don't ferget to call up the job if anybody bothers you. We're open fer business all night ya know. So long!" and Charlie swung himself into the car and dashed noisily away.

Carol went out to the dining room with a sense of leisure upon her that she had not felt since she left New York. A sense of loneliness also. All about her were people in gala attire going somewhere or doing something, and she was stranded in a hotel room. It was Saturday night and she might be having a good time.

But she had no desire to go out of bounds. She would rather be down at that big silent building writing letters and putting careful records in the company books, and straightening out the hopeless tangle of papers that Duskin had allowed to accumulate. She wanted to be watching for the truck to arrive, and to know if it got safely through. Last night at this time Duskin had been rescuing her and now he was perhaps in worse peril and she might do nothing about it but stay in her room obeying his command.

She bought a sheaf of magazines and went up to her room after dinner, but she did not feel like reading. She wrote a long letter to her mother and another to Betty, and racked her brains for things to say without telling the things she knew they would want to hear about, the very things they had warned her of. She took it out in describing the grandeur of the hotel, and the people she saw. She tried to make much of the construction of the great building, showing them what a really beautiful place it was going to be though none of it was quite finished. She spent some time in telling them how much nicer Mr. Duskin was than she had expected, and then she filled out the letter by suggesting a way to make a lovely fall dress for Betty just like one she had seen in a shop window in the hotel. Her own old blue velvet evening dress would do for a blouse, using Betty's last year's blue jersey that had a tear in the sleeve to make a stylish pleated skirt.

When the letters were mailed she tried to read again, but failed to keep her mind on the story she had attempted, and at last she went to bed.

But bed was no place for her active brain. She throbbed all over with excitement. She got to thinking over in detail the events of the night before and suddenly out of the throng of memories came that voice in the dark calling: *Come, Carol!* Who had that been? It had not sounded like Paisley. It had not sounded like Schlessinger, nor even the drunken man, though he couldn't of course have known her name. Who, then, had it been?

It had been a quiet voice, full of comfort, and also command, like Duskin's when he gave orders to his men.

Had Duskin called her *Carol?*

She sat straight up in her bed her cheeks growing hot at the thought.

But why? If he had. How did *he* know her name? Oh, yes, she had signed it to that note she wrote him. Perhaps she ought not to have done that, but—well—anyway—he had not presumed in any other way afterwards. He had been fine, just as if he had been a lifelong friend—or a brother. And perhaps he didn't know he had called her that! Perhaps it had been his subconscious mind that had spoken! Yet—well—

And Duskin was out in the night somewhere, in a world with those same friends who had conspired to take her to that roadhouse last night! They might, they doubtless would like to, do worse by him.

She could stand it no longer. She snapped on the light and called up the building.

After a minute or two Charlie's voice drawled hello.

It came to Carol that somebody alien might be listening in. Silly, perhaps, but possible. She must be guarded in what she said:

"Is that—Charlie?" she asked shyly.

"On the job."

"Have you had any word yet?"

"Not so's you'd know it, ma'am."

"I'd appreciate it if you'll give me a call as soon as you know. I'm not asleep."

"Okay, ma'am. I'll do that little thing as soon as it comes. But you needn't to worry. I know the boys."

She lay down again and tried to sleep but she heard the clock strike one and two and three before she fell asleep, and still no call had come. She had time to thrash her whole life over and face a lot of things during that vigil, and she felt with her last waking thought that she had never really known herself well before.

It was half past seven on Sunday morning that the telephone woke her up, ringing like mad beside her ear. But it was not Charlie's voice that answered her as she voiced a frightened little response into the receiver. It was Duskin's, and it sent a thrill of relief to her troubled heart.

"Good morning, I'm sorry to rouse you so early, but Charlie seemed to think this was the most important next move. I have to report that I arrived safely about five minutes ago. The truck was in bad shape. The lights were bad and held us up for hours. We had to drive so slowly. But we've won through again, and the trim's all ready for Monday morning. I hope you had no trouble."

"Only to worry about the construction engineer," said Carol playfully. "I spent a dull evening in my room marveling on my escape of the night before."

"Be good enough not to stray very far from the hotel today," he said in the tone that she knew meant command. "I don't trust—well—everybody. I'm going to snatch a little sleep this morning, but if you need anyone call Charlie."

"Oh, thank you! I'll be all right," she answered with a lilt in her voice, "I'm going to church across the road. It's a beautiful building and they have a wonderful chime of bells."

"That's good," he said, "I wish I could go too, but I'm afraid I'd disgrace myself going to sleep, in church."

She lay down and thought to go to sleep again, but something glad in her heart kept her awake, and before long she got up and dressed. There was barely time to get some breakfast before the chimes began to ring for service.

Her own head felt a trifle whirly as she sat in the dim sweet light of sunshine that drifted through marvelous old stained glass, and heard the song and prayer and sermon, like faraway bells in her heart! Somehow life looked good to her, she did not know just why, but she was glad that the truck had come through without disaster and the boss was safe at home again. That was enough to make one day bright. How her interest was being bound up in the Fawcett Construction Company! Strange! And she hadn't wanted to come at all!

What was Maine, and the rocks and the sand, and the girls and the excellent hotel? If she were told that she was done here and might start for Maine tomorrow she would not want to go! Now, why was life always contradictory like that?

She spent a good deal of the afternoon reading her Bible, and was amazed to find how interesting it had become. She knew nothing of the revealing power of the great Teacher the Holy Spirit, whom Christ promised should reveal the truth to the seeking heart. She had never read that other promise: "My word shall not return unto me void, but shall accomplish that whereunto I sent it." Nor did she know that her mother, miles away, was at that moment on her knees, praying for her child. Therefore she marveled at the wonders suddenly opening to her eyes.

Monday brought hard work again, and monotony. There seemed to be more men than ever in the building. Carol had to shut her door to keep the sound of their voices from distracting her from her typing. The heater men had arrived with more radiators, great mammoth creatures that took rollers and six men to lift them, and time to get them in. The hall was blocked, the stairs were blocked, the lift could not run because a radiator had slipped across the shaft. The elevator men were held up and began to curse.

Duskin appeared on the scene and restored quiet with a few words and a command or two.

About noon the plumbers arrived. More noise, and more men crawling in and out of small places where pipes like nerves crept all unawares.

Duskin did not get down till three o'clock to sign those letters. He did it breathlessly with strained, tense face and set lips. Carol artlessly asked him why he worked so hard, did he want to break down before the work was over?

He flashed her a keen look, and a few cryptic sentences that made her see that all was not clear sailing yet by any means. The wrong radiators had been sent. This was the second time. They ought to have been in long ago.

When the letters were finished he went to the telephone and Carol had a chance to watch his tired, white face while he talked.

"What? You say those were the ones that were ordered? You are wrong. I was in your establishment Saturday noon. I measured my own consignment which I saw standing ready to be loaded on the trucks. They were the correct ones, just eighteen inches high. They were a special order you will remember, and I went there to make sure that such a mistake could not occur. What? Oh, you think now they must have been shipped elsewhere. Well, that sounds more natural. However, where do you think they were shipped? Kansas City? When? To whom? I'm going to sift this thing down. What? Use these at a discount? No! My contract calls for eighteen-inch radiators, and that is the kind I am going to have. I'm not going to fall down on my contract because you've made a mistake. And I couldn't anyway. The windows are too low to admit any higher radiators. Now, look here, I want my own radiators, and I want them mighty quick! If you can send them over this afternoon and get your men to work at night, and you pay the overtime part, well and good, but if not I'm going to make trouble for you. I know pretty well *who* is paying you to hold up my job, and he isn't going to shoulder the disgrace when it comes out either. *He'll* run away on a fishing trip and let *you* pay the piper, so I advise you to get those radiators over here before five o'clock or I'll get the law on you! I'm tired of chasing you up. You did the same thing about the boilers. I should think you'd try a new trick!"

The right radiators arrived at ten minutes to six, and Carol was amazed and humbled to see a string of heater men walk meekly in a few minutes later and go to work. To think that she had ever thought that Duskin was ineffectual!

But she began to see that he needed to be ten men at least to keep up with the fox who was trying to work his downfall. It evidently was not just plain graft with Schlessinger. It had become a game which he was playing brilliantly, and playing to win at all costs. Too much was involved for him to dare to lose.

Day succeeded day, and to Duskin was much like the night, for he did not pretend to take more than five hours sleep in twenty-four, and often did not get that much.

Carol kept good pace with him, or would have if he had let her. He usually came down and sent her off at six o'clock, or if there was a stress of work and she lingered beyond that he sent Charlie to take her in the car.

Of Duskin himself she saw very little. Once or twice she timed her lunch hour with his and went with him to go to the hot-dog shop because there was something she wanted to ask him. But for the most part she worked her own way through correspondence and accounts without bothering him. If there was something she did not understand she typed her questions and fastened them with a clip to the letter and he answered them when he came to look over the letters.

It was curious how their friendship grew when they had so little contact, a glimpse now and then, a smile, and a word about the work.

Carol had taken over much of the ordering now, and all of the accounts. She signed the vouchers when material was delivered, unless it was something which she was not sure was right and felt Duskin ought to see; only then did she send for him.

He seemed deeply grateful for all this, and he had come to depend more and more upon her, sometimes in very important matters.

"You got a notice this morning that your personal bank account was overdrawn," she said in a matter-of-fact tone one afternoon when he was rushing through his correspondence.

"You don't say," he said looking up worried. "That comes of forgetting to balance my checking account. I really haven't had time. I don't see how—but of course I must have made some mistake."

"Would you care to have me go over it and see what is the matter? I could call up the bank and get them to send up the checks that have come in."

"It would be an imposition to ask you to do that," said Duskin. "I'll try to get time, but I know I shan't."

"It's no trouble to me," said Carol, "it's part of my job you know," she smiled.

"Not to look after my personal discrepancies," he said.

"You looked after mine, once."

"I don't know that that would be called a discrepancy," he said with a grin, "but go ahead if you don't mind. I'll be darned glad to get the thing straight, and I can't take time to do it myself today, that's certain."

He brought her his checkbooks and bankbook from the little private drawer in the safe where he kept his things, and she got to work on it.

She got the bank to send up the checks that afternoon and she pasted them into their respective stubs until everything tallied. But there were some checks which rather amazed her. Dared she speak of them to him? They were undoubtedly what had made his balance so low, for they were for large amounts. One was to a steel company whose name she had never seen before except on a bill of lading for a lot of steel rivets, and a receipted bill which matched the amount of the check. The other was for a lot of paint. The dates were old. They went back to the beginnings of the operation.

While she was fingering over the checks and thinking about it Duskin himself appeared on the scene, on his face the look of a naughty little boy who had come to be punished.

"Did you find out what was the matter? How much am I overdrawn?" he asked her anxiously. "I've been trying to get down again all the afternoon. I ought not to have let this happen. I have a suspicion that Schlessinger is one of the directors of that bank. At least he is thick with them. And he would like nothing better than to trip me up on something like that."

"It isn't a large amount," said Carol thoughtfully, "and I'm wondering whether you didn't make mistakes sometimes and pay things out of your personal account instead of the company account. There are two checks—"

"Yes! I know!" said Duskin and suddenly walked over to the window and began to stare out at the building across the street.

"They aren't mistakes," he said suddenly whirling around and facing her. "Those were a lot of rivets I had to buy because the others didn't get here—*never* got here in fact—Fawcett seemed to think that was a fairy tale, and I hadn't time to write volumes to explain to him, so I paid for them myself. You see we hadn't an account with those folks, and they were—sore about not getting the sale, so they refused to sell except for cash. They were the only people around here who had that many rivets on hand.

"The other check is that lot of paint that was stolen. Fawcett thought that was my fault somehow, or he implied that it was, so I paid for that. But that's all right, or would have been if they hadn't been unreasonably slow in sending me my salary from New York. I thought it would have been here long ago."

"Have they been holding up your salary?" asked Carol in surprise. "That's abominable."

"Well, I thought so myself, but what was the use bothering about it? I had to get this building done, salary or no salary. But now—you don't suppose we could get them to wire some on to me today, do you? I don't see just what I can do. I have friends up in New York I could easily borrow from if I was sure they were home, but the only Chicago friend I have I could ask that favor of has gone to Alaska. Besides, all that would take time."

"Why it's a great deal easier than that," said Carol laughing happily. "I represent the New York office you know, and I have power of attorney. Don't worry anymore about it. I'll straighten it all out. Where are your receipts?"

"Say, that would be wonderful!" he said with a relieved air. "Do you suppose they would okay that? The receipts ought to be around there somewhere in the safe."

"They certainly would," said Carol, "and I'll see that you don't pay for rivets or paint either. Now go back to your work and I'll have everything ready for inspection in an hour. I telephoned the bank that you will send a check over tomorrow morning. Don't worry anymore about it."

Carol investigated the safe and found no vouchers for salary covering the last four months. Could it be possible that the office had been holding him up all that time?

She hunted up Duskin's bankbook, but no deposits had been made during that time either, and on going over his checkbook she found very few checks of late date, and those of pitifully small amounts. He had been running on short rations, bearing his burden bravely, and she had been one of those who had misjudged him and thought him lazy and inefficient. Well, she would see that everybody in the New York office understood now, anyway!

After some thought she put in a long-distance call for New York and got the office just before the treasurer left for the day. He verified the fact that Duskin had not been paid for four months. When she demanded to know why, they told her that Fawcett wanted to investigate things before he let Duskin have any more money, and they had written him to go slow, as they would have to delay his salary. She gave the office to understand that Duskin had been investigated and found to be all that Fawcett could possibly wish. She informed the office that she was giving Duskin his entire salary for the four months, and wished to have them send on the vouchers and straighten out the account. She also was sending in two old accounts which Duskin had paid over a year ago and for which he should have been refunded. She had gone over the specifications and everything was correct. She would verify her conversation by letter that night.

After that she felt better, and Duskin looked like a boy let out of school when he came down and found the check ready for his endorsement.

The next week was the last week of September.

As Carol looked back upon it time seemed to have flown. The number of odds and ends that came to the front at the last minute to be attended to were incredible. Duskin was here and there and everywhere, and never left the building anymore without some of his bodyguard, as Carol called Charlie's gang, following not far off. Duskin wouldn't have allowed it if he had known it, but they arranged it among themselves not to let him out of their sight, and Carol rejoiced that it was so.

Their espionage even extended to her, and she walked the streets when she had to go knowing that someone was likely keeping tab on her comings and goings, and she could not be long away without being looked up.

So they came to the twenty-eighth day of September, late in the afternoon.

"Well," said Duskin dropping down in the other oak chair with a light of accomplishment on his face. "We're all over but the shouting! Charlie and his gang are sweeping out the chips on the third where they had to refit those doors, and the painter is going to touch up a little in the morning. You and I can almost afford to get a sound sleep tonight. Saturday we hand over the keys to the city and we're done! Do you realize that?"

The telephone sounded before she could answer. It was a call for Duskin. When he had finished talking he hurried out.

"I'll be back in half an hour, or sooner," he called. "I've got to get a receipt out of that bird. He thinks it isn't necessary. I sent Pat down for it half an hour ago and he's refused to give it to him."

Carol began to gather up her papers and lock the safe. It was time to go home, but she lingered with the idea of being sure that Duskin came back all right. None of the boys knew that he was out.

Charlie and Ted came downstairs whistling. They were going out to dinner.

"Where's the boss," Charlie asked a trifle anxiously, "I thought he was here. He said he wasn't going out."

Carol explained where he was gone.

"Good night!" said Charlie with a frown, "he needs a lasso, that man! He's bound to have something happen yet if he don't watch out. You gonta stay here awhile, Miss Berkley?"

Carol said that she was.

"All right. I'll just hustle down. I know where Pat went. Likely he's all right but he may need some help. We gotta get all the receipts needed. It's getting dark, and Dusky ought not to be out alone. I saw the long-nosed mayor around this afternoon; he's got back!"

Carol looked up startled.

"You'll be all right, Miss Berkley. Roddy and his bunch are up at the top, and Bill is getting his last onion cooked, don't you smell 'em? We'll be back in no time."

Carol sat down at her desk and began to write out some telegrams she meant to send that night: a long one to Fawcett announcing the completion of the building, and telling in glowing terms of some of Duskin's last triumphs. A night letter to her mother because she hadn't had time to write a letter for several days and she knew they would be worrying. A brief message to the office in answer to one they had sent that day about some technicality.

While she was writing she became conscious that the front door, which had been closed because the day was cool, must have come open; a strong draft blew her papers on the desk.

She looked up to see an old woman with a large bundle tied up in newspaper. She was bent and wore a shawl over her head.

"The boss' laundry," she mumbled. "He told me to leave it back!" She hobbled away down the hall. Carol finished her sentence and then looked up. That was queer! She had never known Duskin to have laundry brought to the job. She got up and went to the door, but the old woman was coming away empty-handed, hobbling cheerfully along.

"I find him," she said, "the old boss, the janitor."

"Oh," said Carol, "you found him, did you?" and she turned doubtfully back and went and watched the old woman from the window. It seemed but a small incident of the day.

While she stood there looking out at the lights that had begun to twinkle in the dusk, she was thinking that it would be only two more nights that she would have to stand so and watch from this window. She wondered what would come next, and how it would seem to go back into her world again. Suddenly she became aware of a sound of padded footfalls along the tiled hall.

She turned sharply about and listened. She was getting nervous. She wished that Duskin would come back. Something might happen even yet. The building was finished, but something might happen to Duskin, in revenge.

She listened, but all seemed to be still, and then she heard the steps again. Had one of the men come down? She stepped to the door and saw a little rubber-soled newsboy idling along from the back of the hall with a stack of papers on his arm.

"What are you doing in here?" she asked severely. He was an uncomely boy, with dirty face and hands and an evil look.

"D'liverin' the janitor's paper!" said the urchin leering at her. "Buy a paper, lady?"

"No," said Carol sharply. "You'd better get out of here. No one is allowed to come in here now the building is finished. The janitor will have to come out and get his own paper after this."

She followed him to the door and shut it decidedly after him, watching him from the window as he sped off down the street calling "Paaaaper! Evnin' paa-per!"

She went back to the desk again but she could not sit still. She went to the window to watch. She wished Roddy and the rest would come downstairs. She was worried and wanted them to tell her everything was all right.

Then suddenly there came to her ears a small snapping, crackling sound. She listened. It couldn't be a mouse, in a great steel and marble structure like that. Of course there was wooden trim and plaster, but a mouse in a new building! That was ridiculous. She turned about and came to the hall door for the third time and as she reached it she thought she smelled smoke. What could Bill be doing that would make smoke? Could something have caught fire in the cellar over his old gas plate? Perhaps he had fallen asleep over his pipe and his dish towel had fallen into the flame. She stepped out into the hall, and the far end near the elevators seemed to be filled with smoke, a fine gray mist. It was curling around from behind the elevators where a stack of leftover trim had been put for the men to take out when the truck came in the morning, and even as she looked she saw a lick of flame leap out into the whiteness of the corridor that was only dimly lighted by one electric bulb at the far end. As if a taunting hand were flung at her she stood helpless.

For an instant it seemed as if her life had leaped to her throat and were choking her. The building they had cherished so and brought to completion! Duskin! It would kill him if anything happened now!

Then she leaped into action.

"Bill!" she screamed. "Bill! Come *quick!* Fire! *Fire!* FIRE!"

She flew down the hall to investigate. The smoke was thicker now, and the flames were leaping up with a roar as they caught the draft from the stairs and elevator shaft, and still no one came! What could she do?

The fire sprinkler that she had watched the men unpack was at the very back of the hall, so near to the flames that one could scarcely get near it without going into the very fire itself. If anyone had indeed started the fire he must have been very cunning. The workmen had been so careful to get every paint rag and cleaning cloth out of the place several days ago. Duskin had spoken of it with relief in his voice. He said that fires started so often from combustion of paint rags. They had not even left a can of gasoline or turpentine around. How could this have happened?

But there was no time to consider. She must do what she could. It would seem that there was no one left in the building.

She screamed again as she went by the elevator, "Fire! *Fire!* FIRE!" but the flames were roaring so now that she could not tell if she was heard. There seemed but one hope of stopping the devastation before it ruined the whole first floor—by smoke if not by burning—and that was the sprinkler. Could she reach it, and if she did could she make it work? She tried to remember as she dashed into the flame, how Duskin had said it must be turned on. Was it to the right, or left?

The flames leaped at her and lashed her face as she went by. She was wearing the little blue jersey frock because the day was cool. She remembered that it was wool and would not catch fire easily. How clearly her brain worked now! She remembered that she ought to have gone to the telephone and given the fire alarm first. But how could she when she wasn't sure there was a fire, and now she was here she must stop it first if she could. There was no time for anything, but she could scream.

She opened her mouth to scream, and the flame leaped out and caught the very words from her lips and stuffed them down her throat with smoke. She gasped as she plunged through, her eyes stung and blinded by smoke, only her hands to feel her way, and find the valve. Was that it? Would it screw around? Was it the right thing?

She was gasping and gripping it with all her might. Something was resulting but she did not know what. She could not get her breath and the thought came to her in a wild spasm that she must get back and call the fire company. She must tell them there were five men up in the tenth story—and Bill down in the cellar. Why didn't someone come? Oh, was she going to faint? She had never fainted in her life. She had always been so proud of that! But the sickening smoke and the heat of the flame, that seemed to be almost licking her face! Was it an eternity she stood there, with that rasping tearing burden on her lungs, and that tang of flame that reminded her of Schlessinger's fox face?

And then she felt the flame subsiding, as if a power greater than itself wrestled with it. She saw it fall back, and lurch forward again, as more and more the sprinkler got control. She could go now, if she could only breathe. If the smoke would clear and the smart in throat and nostrils would give her breath a chance. Would no one ever come?

Why, someone was calling, she must answer!

"Fire!" but it was only a whisper as it came from her smoke-parched lips.

Was that the sound of the boys rushing down from stories above or was she hearing the waves on the shore at the coast of Maine as they boomed against rocks she had never seen? Where was Bill? And where, oh *where* was *Duskin?*

It was her last thought as she drowned away in the smoke. Soul and body and spirit drenched in deadening smoke! They had *got* her and *Duskin* and the *building! The old fox had won!*

Till strong arms gathered her, and bore her out of it all.

She came back again through clear air blowing in her face, and clean water dripping upon her lips and wrists. The electric fan that Duskin had bought one hot day and established near her desk was going at full speed; the windows were open and the blessed coolness was fanning her cheeks.

Somewhere back in her mind a soft voice was singing a verse she had read in her Bible that very morning: "Every word of God is pure; He is a shield to them that put their trust in Him!" And here her God had saved her again! A shield!

She opened her eyes and found that she was lying in Duskin's arms. Duskin's face was watching her eagerly.

"My darling!" he whispered. "Are you all right?"

Charlie was coming in at the door, but she didn't seem to mind. She lay so restfully there in those strong arms. Oh, yes, once before he had held her in his arms, where was that? The fox had been there then. What had she been dreaming? A fire?

Charlie was bringing a glass of ice water. The ice clinked against the glass. He held it to her lips and murmured:

"There, little lady, you drink that, an' you'll feel better!" His tone was so gentle it was funny. He held the glass as if she were a baby, and she wanted to laugh. Duskin's eyes got teary and twinkly, as if he would laugh too only it would hurt Charlie's feelings, but they both understood.

Roddy came in all streaked with soot and water, a great charred stick in his hand.

"Want I should get a doctor-rr, Dusky?" he whispered hoarsely. "It's all out now, every bit."

But Carol lifted her head.

"Is someone hurt?" she asked sharply. "Did the boys get down? Can you stop the fire?"

Then they all laughed, and it was like clear water coming in great streams upon a dry and parched land.

"You put out the fire, little lady," said Charlie when he could speak. "You was just extractin' the last spark when we arrived. Nothin's hurt save old Bill's pride. They trussed him up with some 'lectric wire, and stuffed a old dirty dish towel in his mouth, and left him there to enjoy hisself. He doesn't reckon he'll ever get over not bein' able to help you out, little lady boss!"

"But who did it, and how did it start?" asked Carol, still lying in Duskin's arms and not attempting to rise. It seemed the natural and right thing that she should stay there awhile. They all seemed to expect it.

"Don't ask me," said Charlie. "The old fox himself 'll be at the bottom of it, but who his tool was I can't tell. The same one that telephoned Dusky to go get that receipt, I reckon. He mighta ben sitting there yet ef I hadn't come to take his place. Pat's down there now waiting. We better send someone to redeem that kid. But how they figured it out to get that fire started! We musta had a workman that was yellow—belonged to the other gang, and he knew them trims were piled behind that elevator shaft. It was almost the only stuff in the hall that would burn."

"There was a lot of old rags, all paint, and papers too," added Roddy, "I been examining the ashes."

Then Carol, her eyes very bright, told about the old woman who came with Bill's laundry, and about the insolent newsboy.

Duskin, with his arm still supporting her, looked up gravely:

"Here's where we ask for a little service, boys, and stop this long strain. It was a parting shot, and they'll be disappointed that it didn't work, but I think we can prevent another attempt. Charlie, you get on the phone and call the police headquarters. No, don't tell them what happened. We're not going to let this get into the papers. We're coming out of this clean if we possibly can."

"Is the building spoiled beyond redemption?" asked Carol.

"No," said Roddy crossly, as if he were almost sorry that they didn't have more odds to work against. "Most of it's smoke and will wash off. Some blisters, a little charr-rr-ed wood, a cracked slab or two and some tiles. If we all get to work we can set a lot of it right before morning, and the rest can be fixed tomorrow. Wait till the boss sees it."

"Oh, joy!" said Carol, her strength returning to her. "Let me get up and help. Why, I'm perfectly all right, why do I let you baby me?"

But they would not let her get up. They brought a cot and laid their coats upon it and put her there.

"You can be the boss, little lady," said Charlie smiling, "but you've done enough work for tonight."

Duskin, hardly daring to leave her, had finally gone to the telephone himself, and was marshaling his forces.

"It's double pay to you and your men if you can come down here tonight and fix this up. Yes, double pay, I've said it." His eyes were shining.

He went down the list of men he could trust and sifted out the best, and they came to his call every man of them. Before midnight the place was like a hive of quiet bees, working steadily, each man helping his brother, each intent upon getting the damage hidden from sight, and the clean whole sturdy wall in place again before morning.

Cheerfully the ones who could not work till the others were done, hung around and watched, even taking a hand sometimes when it wasn't in their line of work.

Poor Bill with his pride trailing in the dust like a wet hen's tail, lighted the workers about the cellar, hunting out slabs of marble that had not been used, pieces of trim, timbers, and steel, a bag of cement, plaster and sand and tiles. There seemed to be enough of almost everything, and as the hours went by outside in the dark street a cordon of policemen patrolled the place. And would patrol it until the building was handed over the day after tomorrow to the city, complete and whole.

All night they worked, and when morning dawned there was little left of the devastation that the old laundrywoman with her bundle of soaked rags, and the little snipe of a newsboy with his fatal cigarette had wrought. The old fox would have to sling a bomb over the heads of the whole police force if he wanted to destroy his building now. It stood in the morning sunlight, whole and unscathed.

Inside a few men could be found painting innocently—if anyone forced a way in past the bulldog glare of Bill—but otherwise all things seemed to be about as they had been. There were a few little touches that would be made during the day, but no casual observer would know that anything like tragedy had happened in that hall the night before.

Carol came back the next morning under the protection of Charlie. She wore her rosy dress with her big white cloak and white hat, and they treated her as if she were a queen.

"And what do you think?" she announced to Duskin who looked at her hungrily, and smiled with the look in his eyes she had seen when she first met him, "Mr. Fawcett himself is coming down tomorrow to be at the presentation. The doctor says the good news about the building has put him on his feet. There's the telegram."

She handed it over gaily.

"That may be all right," grumbled Charlie who was hovering around listening, a privileged character, "I'm glad the old boss got well, but it's the lady boss and Dusky that's the real thing, and they oughtta have all the honors."

It was a busy day after all, for they had to get ready to move out, and each one of the gang had to personally look after every other one of the gang all day. And when night came it was with difficulty they persuaded Carol to go back to the hotel and get a good night's rest. It was only because Duskin looked at her gently and told her she must for his sake, that she consented to go.

She was down at the office very early in the morning, all in white, a soft white wool dress, and white hat and coat.

Duskin had had roses sent in, a great sheaf of them, to her.

She wore some of them fastened into the folds of her dress, and arranged the rest around the room in some of Bill's dishes she had found in the cellar.

Duskin wanted to go and meet Fawcett. He felt that it was his place. Carol begged him to stay. She felt that even yet something might happen.

"Nonsense," he said, "they don't want anything more of me now. The building is finished and the day is come. You are here to hold it, and you've plenty of men to stand by you. I'm going to meet Fawcett. It is my place. The job would not be complete without that."

"All right, boss," said Charlie, "I'll go along."

So Duskin and Charlie rode off in the old jalopy to meet the president of the company and Carol stayed behind and waited, with her cheeks growing more like her roses every minute.

So Caleb Fawcett rode up to his finished building on the morning of October first in Duskin's old jalopy that he had bought for fifty dollars, and Carol Berkley, his meek little secretary stood at the doorway to meet him.

"Why, why, my dear little lady!" he exclaimed as he took her hand and looked into her eyes, "Why, you look like a bride! Why, what have you done to yourself?"

He had aged, himself, she thought. His hair was silver about his temples, and his face had been chastened by suffering. But his eyes were as keen as ever, and when he had gone over the beautiful finished building he turned to the two who had followed him anxiously, silently, and said with a voice that was broken with emotion:

"It's beautiful! It's marvelous! I don't know when we've put out a better structure, one that I admired more. And you, my two faithful stewards, I don't know which is to be thanked the most for your faithful devotion and untiring zeal and self-sacrifice. You both deserve all and more than the company can do for you. Duskin, I've been hearing about your amazing selflessness, and almost uncanny powers of accomplishing impossibilities. Every letter this young woman wrote was full of it, even the telegrams—"

He broke off and looked up again at the beautiful, powerful structure.

"Young man, as I look at that building it seems that it has a spirit, the same spirit as your own, indomitable and impregnable."

Suddenly embarrassed at his unwonted flight of imagination, he turned to Carol who was listening in amazement. She had never expected anything like this from her crabby employer:

"And you, my dear little lady! How can I find words to express myself? Your untiring devotion, your heroism! Oh, I've been hearing all about it on the way up from the station!"

Carol was so utterly overcome to hear words like this from her erstwhile hard old boss that she could think of no reply. She could only stand there in wondering embarrassment while his voice went on:

"But, little lady," he was saying, and it sounded as if there were tears in his voice, "you don't know what you did when you had the foresight to take down that evidence! They were planning to make us a lot more trouble and to refuse to make the final payments, on some trumped-up technicality—they've been holding us up on money all along you know—and they meant to lose us the forfeit. It was desperate straits for us because we have a lot of money out elsewhere just now you remember. I got a letter from Schlessinger two days ago threatening the worst. That is what brought me here today. I was wild! But Duskin here met me at the train and told me what you had done, and we called up those crooks before we drove up here, and told them a thing or two. There won't be any trouble now. Schlessinger's a lamb. He's frightened cold! He knows it will be in every paper in the country before night if he doesn't make a clean slate. And it's all on account of you, little lady! We never can thank you enough!"

The peroration was cut short by Schlessinger, suddenly appearing, hurried and apologetic, a scared look in his eyes.

He went through the formalities hastily. He did not even glance at Carol or Duskin. He excused himself as soon as possible and hastened away, professing to have an important meeting to which he was already late.

The rest left the building like a procession with banners, bearing the signed papers, the checks, and their joy.

Duskin, Carol, and Fawcett went in Duskin's car; and the gang followed on the sidewalk, walking solemnly like a bodyguard, as the flivver pursued its leisurely way through traffic.

Fawcett was due to meet his wife at the three o'clock train and go with her to visit her sister in Kansas.

Carol and Duskin saw him off at the train.

He had given them all the praise they could absorb, and two generous checks for a bonus, and they were so happy they did not realize any of it.

They stood arm in arm as if they had always belonged to one another and waved to Fawcett's window as the train moved slowly out of the station.

"And now," said Duskin when it was out of sight, "we're free. Shall we go telephone your mother, or will you take me home and surprise her? I've wanted some folks of my own ever since my mother died, and I'm going to love them a lot. Carol, what would you say to a honeymoon in Maine? They say it is lovely in October. I've never been there, and I've always wanted to go. There are rocks, and sand, and we can watch the waves."

Said Carol with shining eyes, "Let's go back to the hot-dog shop and invite the gang to the wedding! They've been so faithful, and they looked so lonesome when we went away!"

Days afterward, up in Maine, sitting on the sand, watching the waves, Carol was telling Duskin all about the wonderful verses she had found in the Book of Proverbs, and how they had been a lamp to her feet, and a light to show her herself.

Duskin gravely took the book from her hand and turned the pages:

"Ah, but you have forgotten one of the most important, and the most beautiful," he said. "Look! It is in the last chapter. It just describes what by the grace of God has happened to me: 'Who can find a virtuous woman? for her price is far above rubies. The heart of her husband doth safely trust in her.' "